A Crime In The Sixth

A Crime In The Sixth

A PARIS MYSTERY

Eliza Patterson

Full Court Press
Englewood Cliffs, New Jersey

First Edition

Copyright © 2021 by Eliza Patterson

Published in the United States of America by Full Court Press, 601 Palisade Avenue, Englewood Cliffs, NJ 07632 *fullcourtpress.com*

ISBN 978-1-946989-85-7
Library of Congress Control No. 2020924906

Book design by Barry Sheinkopf

This is a work of fiction, and any resemblance to actual persons or places is entirely coincidental.

WITH THANKS TO PATRICIA YOSHA

CHAPTER 1

D AVID LEANED BACK IN HIS DESK CHAIR and smiled at the ceiling. This is it, this is the story that's going to carry me to fame and fortune, he thought to himself. So much for his colleagues and friends who had urged him to stay at his boring job with the *Buffalo News* and called his decision to quit and move to Paris pure folly. "Folly, indeed," he thought, already picturing his Pulitzer Prize. "More like a brilliant career move."

But he had to admit that coming to Paris in fact had not been a strategic career move. Quite the contrary. He had come because he had given up on journalism, and fallen in love. Ever since his first year in J school, he had thought his future lay in investigative reporting. He imagined himself uncovering major crime networks. Professor Jersey, a former investigative reporter himself, had agreed David had "what it takes." He recalled how excited he had been when he was assigned to the local politics beat at the *Buffalo News*. He had been sure that local politics would offer material worthy of investigation. It hadn't. After five years, he had uncovered nothing newsworthy, not even a minor sex scandal, let alone massive corruption. It seemed clear he did not have "what it takes," at least not in Buffalo. So, on September 6, the fifth anniversary of his first day on the job, he had resigned.

"Childish, rash, shortsighted, stupid," had been among the more polite reactions of his friends and colleagues. What they didn't know was that David's grandfather had left him a considerable fortune when he died the year before. Or that he had recently renewed contact with his *petite amie* Micole, from his time at Lycée Henri IV in Paris.

Now, as his gaze shifted from the ceiling to the street outside his window, David silently thanked Micole, for it was really she who had brought him to Paris.

After resigning, David had telephoned to tell her the news. He recalled her reaction verbatim.

"That's terrific! Now you can come help me celebrate. I just won a position as an exhibition designer at the *Fondation Culturespace*. My first job is at the Musée Maillol. I'm working on an exhibit on the collection of Paul Rosenberg. You remember we studied him in our class on *Art Moderne*?"

David smiled. How ironic that he had come to help her but in fact it was she who had helped him. And not only by bringing him to Paris.

At the time, her suggestion that he come visit had been the answer to his most immediate post-resignation concern: what now?

Romance in Paris had seemed the obvious answer. There were no opportunity costs—what would he do in Buffalo?—

and he had money, lots of money, thanks to Grampa Joe.

Shifting his sights back to his desk and his pile of notes and photos, he began to reread the report he had just received from the Desrobert firm. It was the final, crucial piece of evidence.

He got up and poured himself another cup of coffee. Starbucks. Funny that. He remembered, when he first moved to the U.S. for college, he had wrinkled his nose at "American" coffee. "Hot brown water," he'd called it. Now, back in the land of espresso, he favored the big mugs of Starbucks.

He put on a CD of Brahms's *Symphony No. 3* and sat down at his desk to organize his notes and outline his article. *Art Mafia, Alive And Well In The French Capital,* he typed as the tentative headline. As he continued his outline, his thoughts were interrupted by a noise in the front hall.

"Micole, is that you? I thought you weren't coming back until next week."

CHAPTER 2

COMMISSAIRE CLAVEL, A DETECTIVE INSPECTOR of the criminal division of the Paris police, slowly sipped his espresso and watched the clouds drift by over the neighboring tin roofs—the famous *toits-de-Paris*—and mulled over how he would spend his Sunday. The day was unusually mild and sunny for early May. It was too nice to stay indoors, although there was an exhibit at the Musée de la Vie Romantique he wanted to see, but that could wait. Perhaps he should finally take a walk on the new pedestrian promenade along the Seine, appropriately called *Bords de Seine*. He had supported the city's plans to permanently block traffic on that stretch of highway along the Seine. He fancied himself as someone sensitive to "quality of life" issues. He had signed all the petitions of environmental groups and fitness buffs. He had even promised himself he would use the walks and sports equipment on a regular basis to get in shape. He reflected that he was now more than a year older and three kilos heavier, and had never even set foot on the promenade. Well, that would change today, he told himself, and reached for a second croissant. He'd walk off the calories. He put his dishes to soak in the sink—washing up, like exercise, was something Clavel tended to postpone—and was digging out his comfortable shoes when the phone rang.

Who could be calling at 10:00 a.m. on a Sunday? Maybe his cousin inviting him to lunch. Cecile was a great cook, and their garden would be at its peak. No, he needed exercise, and he could visit another time.

"*Oui, allô.*"

"Commissaire, it's Inspector Jean-Paul. We've had a call from a hysterical women claiming to be a '*gardienne,*' who says there was a break-in and an unconscious man in one of her apartments—a David Barber, an American."

"Can't you send Hubert?"

"No, sir, he is on paternity leave. I'm the only one here and can't leave the phones unattended."

"Paternity leave? All this gender equality is getting out of hand."

"Yes, sir, but. . . ."

"OK, OK. Did you call an ambulance?"

"Yes, sir, and I'm told they have taken the victim to the hospital."

"Where is the apartment?"

"Sixteen, rue Cassette, in the sixth, near place Saint-Sulpice."

"Right, tell Madame Whatever I'll be there in five minutes."

Clavel rushed down the circular stairs from his sixth-floor apartment and headed down the rue des Martyrs in search of a taxi. He shook his head in disbelief at the number of twenty-somethings crowded into the chic cafés. The neighborhood, like the police force with its paternity leave, certainly had changed since he moved there thirty-three years before following his divorce. Then, on a typical Sunday, the rue des Martyrs would have been lined with trucks selling farm produce to the neighborhood's *petits bourgeois*. Folks who preferred a *petit rouge* to a *latte,* and a *baguette* to an organic *"pain fantaisie."* His favorite *boulangerie* had closed the previous month when the baker and owner M. Lafolle retired. Same story for Mme Patti, the green-grocer. At least La Poulard Saint-Honoré butcher shop with its vast selection of meats was holding on. If they closed he'd have to move too, or take to eating prepared dishes in plastic cartons from the numerous take-out shops. He shivered at the thought.

He was glad to see a taxi waiting at the stand next to the church Notre Dame de Lorette. He wondered how long that would last as Uber took the city by storm. Rousing the sleeping driver, he foolishly flashed his police credentials and said he was in a hurry. The driver took this as permission to play race-car driver. Fortunately, the streets were relatively empty and they arrived in one piece in a record-breaking fifteen minutes. He generously tipped the grinning driver, wondering if he wasn't encouraging reckless driving.

Rue Cassette was considered to be among the most desirable addresses in the city. Located in the heart of the prestigious Sixth arrondissement, residents had easy access to the Luxembourg Gardens, St. Germain art galleries, upscale boutiques, cafés, and restaurants. Realtors undoubtedly promoted it as a place occupied by *"des gens biens"*—respectable people. Yes, thought Clavel with distaste, no ethnic or economic diversity here.

Number 16 was, similar to many buildings in the area, a well-maintained ashlar stone building accessible only to those knowing the entry code or being buzzed in. Not knowing the code, Clavel rang the shiny brass bell. The door was opened immediately by a woman who was clearly expecting him and introduced herself as "Madame Langel, the *gardienne."* Had she not done so, he would have assumed she was an owner. The initial impression was of someone of means for whom personal appearance was of utmost importance. She was tall and thin with high cheekbones, large almond-shaped eyes and an almost lipless mouth. Her thick auburn hair, cut short with a long fringe, was clearly the work of an expert and expensive coiffeur. Clavel judged her to be in her mid-sixties. She was wearing a tailored navy blue suit and matching high-heeled blue shoes. The only hint of her occupation was her hands. They were large and rough-skinned. The rings and manicured nails could not disguise the fact that they were hands that had done their share of cleaning. They did indicate, however, that today someone else was responsible for the clean floors and polished brass.

Had she been hysterical when she called headquarters, as Jean-Paul had claimed, she had calmed down. "This way," she said, with a welcoming gesture toward the stairs. Her demeanor was more that of a receptionist at a five-star hotel welcoming a newly arrived guest, than of someone who had just discovered a gruesome crime. There's something wrong with this picture, thought Clavel.

The apartment was just one flight up and occupied the entire floor. The wide circular staircase with its stained glass windows and polished mahogany rail reinforced Clavel's sense of being in a high-end hotel.

The illusion was shattered on entering the apartment. A tornado could not have created more havoc. The apartment was composed of a small entry hall, a large living-dining room, a small old-fashioned kitchen, and two bedrooms.

The floors were strewn with clothes, papers, emptied drawers, and broken picture frames. Reigning over the chaos from one corner of the living room was a magnificent Biedermeier kneehole desk. Clavel had one himself and wondered if the victim had also found it at an antique store in the Saint-Ouen flea market. Refocusing on the task immediately at hand, Clavel walked over to the desk, being careful not to touch any of the objects on the floor. The seven drawers had all been removed and lay next to the desk. On top were three twenty-euro bills and a Crédit Agricole credit card. A simple robbery this was not. The intruders clearly were looking for something, but what?

The piles of papers left on the floor would be of little help other than as an indication of what they had not been interested in. Clavel would delegate the tedious task of examining them to his forensics team and crime scene operatives. Hopefully, they would be able to get some fingerprints or stray hairs and fiber, which would help in identifying the intruder or intruders. So too might the lingering odor of pipe smoke. That, however, he'd have to remember. As a long-time pipe-smoker, Clavel had developed a fine-tuned nose for the various scents of different tobaccos. This scent was one with which he was not familiar, but it wasn't one he'd forget.

Clues as to motive were more likely to come from information about the victim. From the brief description he had received, it seemed clear the man was in no shape to tell his own story—and might never be. A typical concierge could be a source of useful information. In his experience, they tended to know far more about the residents than those residents recognized or would have liked. But Clavel suspected that Mme Langel might be less forthcoming than most, albeit perhaps more informed. She had made it quite clear she was a *"gardienne"* and not a *"concierge"*—the latter term being synonymous with gossip.

As puzzling as motive was opportunity. How did the intruders get in? he wondered. There was no sign of forced entry, and Mme Langel had already said she had neither seen nor heard anything unusual. The bedrooms looked over a narrow alley that was used to store garbage cans. Clavel reflected that, if a person stood on the cans, they could easily climb into the window. The windows were shut and not broken, but every petty thief in Paris knew how to open these casement/French door windows. Another possibility was that the culprit had a key.

"If you have a moment, I'd like to ask you a few more questions."

"Of course, if you'll come to my loge. I'm expected to be present at this hour." Clavel sensed a note of resentment in the latter phrase.

Even having met its occupant, Clavel was stunned by the apartment—indeed, "loge" did seem an inappropriate term for this elegant space.

When he just joined the force, an older colleague had counseled him to pay attention to people's homes—furniture, decor, trinkets can tell you a lot about a person. This was certainly true of his own sparsely furnished, functional, messy, apartment, in which the only noteworthy objects were his two guitars, a top-of-the-line stereo system, and an impressive collection of cassettes—mostly classical but some jazz. It screamed "music-loving bachelor." Yet he wasn't sure how to read the flat he had just entered. It was odorless, as if no one lived there.

He had seen many concierge loges during his years on the police force and had found them uniformly drab. Utilitarian would be an apt description of the decorating style. Typical would be a sturdy wood dining table covered with a plastic tablecloth, a well-worn dark-colored sofa, and an overstuffed easy chair or two. Pictures were generally of pastoral or religious scenes. And the floors either highly polished and bare or covered with inexpensive, easy-to-clean, throw rugs.

Mme Langel's flat could not have been more different. It

was anything but drab. He guessed it was the work, recent work, of a professional interior designer. The rugs were fine Orientals, the furniture ultra-modern—all chrome and glass and black leather—and on the walls were several large oil paintings which reminded Clavel of ones he had seen recently at Musée Pompidou; the names Braques and Matisse came to mind, but he wasn't sure, his knowledge of art being sadly limited. There was nothing even remotely personal here. There were no books, no family pictures. Other than the Oriental rugs, everything appeared brand new. And he suspected the rugs were recent purchases. It looked more like the showroom of a high-end furniture store than a home.

"Please, have a seat. Would you like some coffee?"

Clavel would have preferred something stronger but graciously accepted. He was glad he had. The coffee was excellent, strong, and topped with the thick *crema* so key to a good espresso. He guessed she had the latest Nespresso machine.

He would have liked to ask her about herself but knew he had no right to do so and hoped personal information would slip out in the course of a well-designed conversation. His charm was going to be put to the test.

"The coffee is excellent," he said with a broad and, he hoped, not transparently fake smile. "When did you first become aware that there was a problem?"

"As I already told your colleague, when Madame Corez, from the third floor, came down and told me she was worried about Monsieur Barber. She said they had agreed to have coffee at ten, and he didn't answer his bell. I don't like to disturb owners but Madame Corez insisted, so I went up to see. When no one answered, I used my master key to go in and found Monsieur Barber lying next to the door and the room as you saw it. I immediately called the police."

"And you had heard nothing?"

"No."

"And you have seen no signs of forced entry?"

"No."

"Do you have any idea who could be responsible?"

"No."

"Are you aware of any animosity between the victim and other owners?"

"Certainly not. I don't spy, and the people in this building are not the type to commit violence."

"You said you used the master key to enter the apartment this morning. Do you know who else, other than Monsieur Barber, had a key to his apartment?"

"No. How would I know who he chose to give keys to? Of course, I would not be surprised if his *petite amie* didn't have one. She was always coming and going—she almost lived here," she said, shaking her head in disapproval.

"*Petite amie*? Do you happen to know her name or how I could contact her?"

"No. Monsieur Barber was a very private person. We rarely spoke."

Clavel wasn't surprised. Mme Langel was not the sort of person who encouraged intimacy. "Were the locks changed before Monsieur Barber moved in?"

"No."

"So anyone to whom the prior owners might have given keys would have continued to have access?"

"Yes, yes, of course," she said as if the thought pleased her.

"Do you know if either they or David employed someone to clean their apartment?"

"I'm sure not. I would have noticed had someone come regularly."

Clavel had the impression that the question made her uneasy. An almost imperceptible change in her attitude, but one he'd noticed.

"Thank you for your time and for the delicious coffee," said Clavel, rising to leave. "You have been most helpful." *Not!* he thought. "I'll just go speak with Madame Corez."

Mme Langel looked as if she were about to object but, before she could do so, Clavel walked out and rang for the elevator. He knew he should walk up—it was only three flights—but he was feeling lazy. His resolve to get in shape could wait.

The door to Mme Corez's flat was ajar. She was obviously waiting for him.

"Come in, come in, Commissaire," came a soft voice in response to his knock. This was likely to be a more hospitable environment, thought Clavel. And hopefully a more productive discussion.

"I'm sorry to disturb you, but I have just a few questions."

"Certainly, certainly. Do sit down. I'll just bring some coffee," said the voice from inside the apartment.

More coffee he did not need but appreciated the warm welcome and was grateful to have a few moments to himself to examine the apartment. The room facing the front door was large and served as both living and dining room. Old money, speculated Clavel. Above the fireplace to his right was a large mirror with an elaborate curvilinear wood frame. In it were reflected three oil paintings in gilt frames. One wall was occupied entirely by a dark wood bookshelf on which leather-bound books were arranged, seemingly by size. The wall facing him as he entered was divided by three large, sparklingly clean French windows giving onto a balcony. The floor had a few scattered Oriental rugs, leaving sufficient space to show off the elegant *point de Hongrie* flooring. The sofa and chairs were notable for the elaborate floral shapes of the legs and backs. Facing the sofa was a low coffee table on which there were three large art books—one on stained glass windows, one on Art Nouveau, and one on French cathedrals. In some contexts, the books would have appeared to be "displayed," but here they seemed to reflect a genuine interest on the part of the owner and to have actually been read. Clavel picked up the book on Art Nouveau and, flipping through the pages, recognized much of the furniture in the room. Mme Corez seemed to have an interest in the arts. His speculation was interrupted by the appearance of Mme Corez bearing a silver tray with a French-press coffee pot, a silver sugar bowl, and two bright yellow espresso cups.

Had she been poor, she would undoubtedly have been called ugly but, with the help of a talented hairdresser and careful makeup, she was stunning. She was petite, had a long, thin, pointed nose, small hazel eyes, and a generous, expressive mouth. Her curly, thick brown hair was professionally streaked with blond and was cut to just below her ears. She was wearing casual but well-fitting beige pants and a loose brown and white top.

"I assume you have come to ask about poor David. Is he going to be OK? I can't understand what happened. I've lived here for almost thirty years, and we have never had any problems. And David was such a quiet, well-mannered young man."

Ah, yes, all *'des gens biens,'* thought Clavel.

"I understand it was you who discovered the break-in."

"Yes, I had arranged to stop by for coffee at ten. We had coffee together frequently. He was interested in knowing about Pierre and Irene, Monsieur and Madame Maren—they were the prior owners and dear, dear friends of mine. He had asked me to come today specifically to talk about their art collection."

"Did you mention this meeting to anyone?"

"No. Oh, yes, I did mention it to Monsieur Lotan—he lives upstairs. We had arranged to go for a walk at eleven and I thought I might be late."

"You said David was interested in the former owners. Had he met them?"

"Yes, he knew Pierre. Irene died several months before David bought the apartment. It was a *viager* purchase."

"*Viager?*"

"Yes, are you not familiar with this type of sale?"

"No, sorry."

"It's a special type in which the seller sells his apartment in exchange for monthly payments while continuing to occupy the apartment until his death. I didn't like the idea at all, and I told Pierre so. Why would you want to provide a total stranger a reason to wish you dead as soon as possible? But Pierre was set on the idea. He told me he wanted to live in style and couldn't afford to do so on his pension. The apartment was his only significant asset, and he didn't want to move and had no interest in leaving the apartment to Irene's children or anyone else."

"Irene's children?"

"Ah, yes—you see, Irene had been married before to a Russian named Novochkin, and Olivier and Monique were from her first marriage. They were both adults when Pierre and Irene married and, according to Irene, opposed the marriage."

"Why was that?"

"Apparently they thought Pierre was a gold-digger. Which of course is ridiculous. Certainly Pierre, an academic with a modest salary, was less well off than Irene, but she was hardly wealthy."

"And where are the children now?"

"Monique married an American, a professor I think, and moved to the U.S. I don't know where. Olivier works at a designer boutique not far from here—Peggy Huyn. I'm not sure in what capacity."

"Do you know when David purchased the apartment?"

"Yes, a little less than a year before Pierre died."

"And during that time David got to know Pierre? Do parties to *viager* contracts generally socialize?"

"I have no idea, but David seemed eager to do so. I remember Pierre telling me that he came to visit the day after the sale bringing flowers and asking if he could take pictures of the apartment to show his friends. After that, he came by at least once a week. Pierre was rather a shy person but he seemed to take to David immediately. Perhaps, for Pierre, David was the son Olivier refused to be."

"Did David also know Olivier?"

"I'm sure not. Olivier was very bitter about his mother's second marriage. He was not a frequent visitor after the marriage. He seemed to make a point of shunning Pierre—rather childish, I think."

"Do you think either Olivier or the daughter resented Pierre's having sold the apartment in *viager?*"

"Goodness, no. It was Pierre's apartment from before his marriage to Irene, and they knew they didn't have a chance at inheriting it."

"You said David wanted to speak with you about an art collection."

"Yes. Pierre, or rather Irene, had a collection of paintings that were auctioned on Pierre's death."

"And you were familiar with the collection?"

"Oh, yes, you could say our friendship was founded on the collection. I met Irene at the Russian Orthodox Church several years before she married Pierre. It turned out we had much in common. Both our fathers were art collectors in Russia. They both fled during the revolution of 1917, after having most of their collections confiscated by the authorities. My family lost everything, but according to Irene, the authorities didn't bother to take a handful of her family's paintings, judging them to be of little value. Irene, an only child, inherited the much-diminished collection. Over the years she continued to collect, but mostly unknown artists. She told me, half jokingly, that she hoped she had her father's 'eye for value' and that her purchases would prove to be good investments, because it was all she had to leave her children. She told me her will provided that, on her death, all the art would go to Pierre for his life, but when he died the collection was to be auctioned with the proceeds going to her children."

"Why auctioned?"

"I gather she thought it would avoid fights between the two children over who got which work. The proceeds could be split evenly."

"Would the amount have been substantial?"

"I don't know. I didn't attend the auction, but I doubt it. None of the works struck me as particularly noteworthy. Based on my own family's experience, the Soviets knew their art and generally took everything of value and, between us, I don't think Irene had 'an eye for value.'"

"When was the auction?"

"It was at Drouot, about a week after David moved in."

"Did David attend?"

"Yes, he told me later he had purchased one of the paintings. He seemed very pleased with himself."

"Did he tell you which work he had purchased?"

"No."

Clavel jotted a note to have Claire see what she could find out. He assumed someone kept lists of purchases.

"You have lived here a long time, I understand," said Clavel, switching topics.

"Yes, over thirty years."

"Do you know the other owners? I assume all the units are owner-occupied?"

"Oh, yes, we've all been here forever—until David arrived it was almost a retirement home," chuckled Mme. Corez.

"Pierre and Irene had the first floor. Monsieur Miceli and his sister live on the second. I'm on the third. Madame Barton, a retired librarian, is on the fourth, and Monsieur Lotan, a retired doctor, is on the fifth."

"And the concierge?"

"You mean the *gardienne*?" asked Mme Correz with a smile and a wink.

Clavel reciprocated in kind, hoping to encourage as much scuttlebutt as possible.

"She started working here just before my husband passed away—that was five years ago now."

"Do you know anything about her past?"

"Only that she had been a concierge in Lyon before coming to Paris and had good references."

"You mean a *gardienne*?"

"No, in fact she only recently changed her title to *gar-*

dienne—including on the mailbox, you may have noticed."

"When was that?"

"Let me see, it was after Pierre died and just a few weeks before David moved in, because the two mailboxes were re-labeled on the same day."

"Did you notice any other changes at the time?"

"Oh, yes. It was rather extraordinary. We—I and the other residents, that is—assumed she had received an inheritance. She had the entire apartment redecorated. Several residents complained at the noise and mess caused by the movers, but I think she had as much right as anyone else to redecorate. She redecorated herself as well—I'm sure you noticed her clothes."

"Well, I admit I was a bit surprised by her appearance, and that of the loge."

"Tut-tut, *apartment*," winked Mme Corez.

Clavel was becoming fond of Mme Corez. She had a wicked streak that reminded him of his mother.

"And you say all these transformations happened at about the time Monsieur Barber moved in?"

"Oh, my, are you implying that Madame Langel's good fortune could have something to do with David? Is she a suspect?" asked Mme Corez, slumping back into her chair. She seemed genuinely surprised and worried.

"Everyone is a suspect at this point. It's simply important that I know as much as possible about everyone who had anything to do with Monsieur Barber."

"Am I a suspect?" asked Mme Corez, who seemed to have regained her composure and sense of humor.

"Of course," said Clavel with what he hoped was his most engaging smile. Mme Corez was proving to be a valuable source—so far, his only one—and he needed to be sure she remained one.

"About Madame Langel. You say you and the other residents assume she received an inheritance. In other words, she has offered no explanation?"

"No, none. Of course, no one asked her."

"Did she mention a funeral, or show signs of mourning a loss?"

"No. But she never was very communicative. I really know nothing about her."

"No family or regular visitors?" asked Clavel, hoping to get a clearer picture of the intriguing *gardienne*.

"Not that I'm aware of. Of course, I don't spy on her, and I wouldn't be aware if someone came unless I happened to be in the hall at the time."

"Was she on equally distant terms with everyone in the building?"

"Yes, when she first came, we all noticed the contrast with Madame Suarez, the prior concierge, a real chatterbox. The only person she ever said more than two words to was Pierre. I think that was because he paid her, a lot, to clean his apartment once a month after Irene died."

"She was his cleaning woman?" asked Clavel with obvious surprise. The role seemed out of keeping with her apparent self-image.

"I'm sure she would reject that title, but yes. Pierre was

helpless and, when Irene died, I suggested he hire someone to clean and cook for him. He refused to hire someone to cook but after a few months admitted he needed help cleaning and hired Madame Langel. Knowing Pierre, he probably described the position as 'house manager,'" giggled Mme Corez.

"I would like to know more about your mysterious *gardienne*. Do you know where I could find a copy of her letter of recommendation, or at least the name of her former employers?"

"I don't remember the details—age does that to the brain—but I'm sure George—Monsieur Lotan—has the letter. He is the self-appointed keeper of documents for the tenants' association. As a doctor, I guess he's in the habit of keeping records."

"Thank you, Madame Corez, you have been extremely helpful, and I don't want to take more of your time today," said Clavel, rising to leave.

"Would you like me to introduce you to Monsieur Lotan? I'm sure he's in now—he rarely goes out on Sunday."

"Thank you, I would," said Clavel.

"Just let me change my shoes, and I'll take you up."

When she reappeared, she was wearing a pair of chic patent leather pumps and had clearly spruced up her makeup.

"Shall we walk up? Monsieur Lotan says there is nothing like climbing stairs to keep in shape," she said, smiling.

"Absolutely."

Rather than ring the bell, Mme Corez gave three rapid knocks.

"It's our code," laughed Madame Corez.

The door was opened immediately by a tall, distinguished gentlemen. His white hair was cut long and brushed back, revealing a high forehead and large blue eyes. His large, fleshy lips gave him a somewhat feminine appearance. Clavel judged him to be in his mid-seventies and noted somewhat resentfully that he was in superb physical shape. He was wearing gray flannel trousers and a tight, pale gray turtleneck that revealed his well-toned muscles.

"Bonjour, Dominique," he said, kissing her on both cheeks in the traditional French *bises*.

"Georges, this is Commissaire Clavel. He's in charge of the break-in and assault of Monsieur Barber."

"Do come in, Commissaire. How can I be of assistance?"

"He would like to see a copy of the letter of recommendation of Madame Langel. You do have it, don't you, George?" answered Mme Correz before Clavel could open his mouth

"Yes, of course. But of what possible interest could it be?"

"Probably none," Clavel explained, "but I would like to know a bit more about her. I understand she underwent a rather significant transformation just after Monsieur Barber—David—moved in. The two events may be unrelated, but the timing raises questions."

"Yes, yes, I guess it would. I'll just get the folder."

The letter was a standard recommendation letter specifying that Mme Langel had been the concierge for the building in Lyon for five years and performed to their entire satisfaction; they were sad to see her leave but respected her decision to move to Paris. Clavel was disappointed that no mention was made of why she had decided to move, but there was nothing surprising about the omission. He noted the address and phone number of the former employers and returned the letter to the doctor.

The doctor had not asked Clavel or Mme Corez to sit down, which surprised Clavel. It was out of keeping with the doctor's obvious fondness for "Dominique," as well as with generally accepted norms of polite behavior.

If the doctor had hoped they would leave quickly, he was going to be disappointed, thought Clavel, casually taking a seat on the large black leather sofa.

Out of the corner of his eye he noticed the doctor giving Mme Corez a questioning look to which she replied with a shrug as she joined Clavel on the sofa. The doctor chose a matching black leather easy chair. Clavel thought he had seen one just like it at a Christie's auction recently, estimated at €20,000–30,000.

"May I be of further assistance, Commissaire?" he asked with a not too discreet glance at his watch.

"I hope so," said Clavel, flipping his notebook to a clean page. "Regarding Madame Langel. What do you know about the source of her recent good fortune?"

"Absolutely nothing. She is the building's concierge. Her private life is of no interest to me."

"*Gardienne*," interjected Mme Corez with a hint of a smile.

"Ah, yes, *gardienne*," said the doctor, rolling his eyes.

No interest, not no business, mused Clavel—the doctor

was revealing himself to be a snob. Someone his mother would have said "opposed mixing the linen with the rags."

"You didn't find the change surprising? Didn't congratulate her in the hopes of eliciting an explanation?"

"No. We rarely spoke."

"How well did you know David?" inquired Clavel, switching topics and hoping the young man's social status merited the interest of the doctor.

"Not well. We had coffee together several times at Dom— at Madame Corez's," he said, nodding in her direction. "I enjoyed his company. He had a contagious *joie de vivre*. Energetically optimistic would be an apt description. A welcome contrast to the morose French youth."

"Did you ever visit him in his apartment?"

"No, I was never invited and wouldn't expect to be."

"Can you think of any reason someone would wish him ill?"

"None at all, but I would assume the motive was robbery and David was merely collateral damage."

"Collateral damage," a cold-hearted way of putting it, thought Clavel.

"In that case, why do you think they chose his apartment and not another? I would imagine other apartments offered greater bounty," said Clavel, gesturing to the contents of the room. Doing so, he noticed a rack of some ten pipes on the

"Are you a pipe-smoker, Doctor?"

"More a collector of pipes than a smoker, but yes, I do indulge from time to time," answered Lotan, obviously surprised by the abrupt change of topic.

"A secret he keeps from his patients," added Mme Corez, fondly patting his hand.

"Your secret is safe with me," said Clavel, although he planned to find out more about the doctor's habit.

"I understand you have lived here a long time. What can you tell me about the former owners—the Marens?" continued Clavel, again shifting topics. He found it a good way to keep his interlocutors off balance.

"What do you want to know? We were not close friends, but as neighbors we were on amicable terms."

"Had you seen their art collection?"

"No, but I understand from Madame Corez that it didn't really merit the term 'collection.'"

"You certainly have an impressive collection yourself," remarked Clavel, rising to get a closer look at the row of large oils in gilt frames.

"Is this a Chagall?" he asked, hoping his memory of the Chagalls on the ceiling of the Opéra Garnier was accurate and that he was not too off base.

"No, it's a Tobiasse. Many people make the same mistake."

"It's wonderful. Did you buy it in Paris?"

"No, in Geneva."

"Who's the artist here?" asked Clavel, pointing to a small oil depicting a harbor with sailboats.

"Marquet."

"It's lovely. When did he paint?"

"Early twentieth century; he was part of the Fauvist movement. I appreciate your interest in art, Commissaire, but I'm rather busy."

"Yes, yes, I'm sorry, but your collection, and I'm sure it merits the term, is like a museum. Well, I don't need to take any more of your time, but if you think of anything that might shed some light on the issue, please contact me," said Clavel, rising and handing the doctor his card.

"Yes, of course," replied the doctor with a slight bow of the head as he opened the door.

Mme Corez accompanied Clavel out.

Although the doctor had said nothing very surprising, he had captivated Clavel's interest. He was sure the man was a player, maybe an important one, in the Barber case. Luckily, an obvious source of information about him was standing by his side.

"The doctor certainly has an eye for art. I assume the paintings are all originals," said Clavel to Mme Corez as they walked down toward her apartment.

"Oh, yes, George—Monsieur Lotan, he dropped the title doctor when he retired—is quite an expert, particularly in twentieth-century artists—like the Fauves he mentioned. Now that he is retired, he spends his time at art fairs and auctions."

"Does he sell as well as buy?"

"Yes. I joke that he is more a trader than a collector. He often buys works at one fair and sells them at another or to a gallery without ever hanging them on his walls."

"He must be a true expert. It's a risky market."

"I guess it's in his blood. His father owned a gallery and his mother was a sculptor—not a very successful one, I gather."

"Do you think he might give me some advice? I saw a painting in a gallery on rue de Seine recently that I would love to have, but it's expensive and, for all I know, junk."

"I can't promise, but he has given me some tips."

The five bells of Saint Sulpice chimed 2:00 p.m. just as Clavel was saying good-bye to Mme Corez, signaling that it was time for something more substantial than coffee. It was also time he got back to the office to see what if anything the crime scene team had come up with. The pizza place he had noticed on the corner seemed an obvious solution. Except it wasn't. He hoped the pizzas justified the name "Pizza Chic," because the prices certainly did. "Twenty euros and up for a small pizza," Clavel mumbled to himself in disgust as he looked around for other options. Seeing nothing but real estate offices and a boulangerie, he resigned himself to having a sandwich. He was glad he had. The camembert and chicken on a baguette and the *baba au rhum*, which he ate sitting by the fountain on the place Saint Sulpice, surpassed his expectations. The bread was chewy and the cheese ripe but not so strong as to overwhelm the chicken. And they hadn't skimped on the rhum, as was too often the case with commercial babas.

As Saint Sulpice chimed 3:00, Clavel rose reluctantly and headed to his office on the quai des Orfèvres to review the findings of the crime scene investigators.

CHAPTER 3

O N HIS DESK WERE THE INVESTIGATORS' REPORT and three neatly arranged stacks of loose papers the investigators had found in the apartment. There was also a note from his secretary Mme Pinan saying a Doctor Botlan had called and asked that Clavel call him; it was about David Barber. He dialed the number and to his surprise was directly connected to the doctor.

"Commissaire, thank you for calling. I understand you are in charge of the investigation into the assault on David Barber. I wanted to let you know that he has suffered quite severe head injuries and remains unconscious. I don't think his life is in danger, but, given the particular nature of the injury, he may suffer from amnesia, perhaps permanently. Given the precision with which the head was struck, and the fact that no other injuries were inflicted, I think it quite likely the assailants specifically intended to cause amnesia."

"Thank you, Doctor, that is extremely valuable information. I assume you will let me know about any developments in his condition."

"Of course."

Turning back to the papers on his desk, he noticed that on top of one of the stacks was a computer cord and a business card. The card was that of Marc Lafitte of the Art Deco gallery on rue de Miromesnil.

According to the report, the investigators had found the cord under a bunch of clothes. Stupid to have left the cord, thought Clavel. It was pretty good evidence that they had taken a computer and, having left cash, it was unlikely they did so for its resale value.

The card had been found jammed between the back of the Biedermeier desk and the wall. The attackers had emptied and removed the drawers but apparently not thought to move the desk. The card was left because it wasn't found, not because it wasn't relevant. God bless carelessness, thought Clavel.

According to the card, the gallery in the ritzy Eighth arrondissement was open on Sunday afternoons. No time like the present.

"Jean-Paul," he called through the open door.

"*Oui, chef?*" said junior officer Jean-Paul, who appeared immediately as was appropriate for his relative status.

Clavel made a point of not pulling rank, but the habits of hierarchy were well ingrained in the police force.

"I'm going to the Eighth to interview a gallery owner who knows our victim. Monday morning first thing, I want to meet with you and Luc—assuming he's not on leave of some kind. We need to develop a plan of action for this Barber case."

"Barber?"

"Yes, sorry, that's the surname of our victim—David Barber."

"Right, have a nice evening, sir."

Unlikely, thought Clavel. He disliked the Eighth arrondissement. It was populated by people like those with whom he had grown up—rich, arrogant and self-satisfied. People he disliked and with whom he felt ill at ease. He had tried to flee by enrolling in the police academy rather than Sciences Po or one of the prestigious universities known as "Grands Écoles," as had his classmates. And he had married, over the objections of his mother, the niece of a fellow police cadet. He had never regretted either choice. Neither did he regret having settled in the working class Ninth arrondissement. In fact he regretted it was "gentrifying"—the term favored by local realtors.

The Eighth was and remained the playground of his former classmates, and whenever he walked down the rue de Rivoli or Faubourg Saint-Honoré, he pushed his hat over his face to avoid being recognized. He had no interest in repeating an encounter he had had early in his career. He recalled the incident as if it were yesterday. He had been standing at the bar of a café on rue de Surène, drinking an espresso, when a voice called out—"Maurice." Turning, he saw two of his former classmates seated at a table in the back of the room. Dressed in well-tailored suits and starched white shirts, they looked like a movie version of young successful politicians or businessmen—which is certainly how they thought of themselves. They had beckoned him to join them." You don't have to stand.

We'll treat you to a seat," said one, "and even a croissant," laughed the other.

"Thank you, but I have to leave," answered Clavel, looking at his watch. "I have a meeting." It wasn't true, but he wanted to get away as quickly as possible.

"Ah, well, I guess policemen can't dawdle. Shame, but take my card. If you ever need anything—a loan or a recommendation—let me know," said one, glancing mockingly at his friend.

Clavel wished he had found a stinging reply and was ashamed to have slunk out like a wounded dog. He also knew he'd react the same way were the incident to repeat itself, and so avoided the Eighth to the extent possible. Which, unfortunately, was not the case today. As he put on his coat, he decided it would be best to call first. The card indicated the gallery was open on Sunday but that was no guarantee.

"Bonjour, Monsieur Lafitte?"

"Speaking."

"This is Commissaire Clavel of the police judiciare, brigade criminelle. I wonder if I could stop by to speak with you this afternoon?"

"Commissaire? Police? What is the problem?" asked Lafitte in the nervous tone calls from the police usually triggered.

"I'd like to speak to you about a David Barber. I gather you know him?"

"Yes, I do. What's happened? Has his investigative reporting landed him in trouble?"

"He's been assaulted." Clavel preferred to wait to provide further details until he could observe Lafitte's reaction.

"You're kidding, right?"

"No, I'm not. May I come and see you?"

"Of course, of course, I'm in the gallery, rue de Miromesnil just next to Beauvau—the Ministry of the Interior. I'll be here until seven."

Clavel knew what Beauvau was. Why did people assume policemen were uneducated? Or was it something about the Eighth arrondissement?

The gallery was typical of the area—small but offering large-ticket items. As its name implied, it specialized in Art Deco—furniture, paintings, and sculpture. A fan, Clavel's mouth watered. The collection was magnificent. If he'd followed the path of his former classmates, he might be here as a client rather than an investigating cop. Damn Eighth, it aroused nothing but negative feelings.

He shook his head, hoping to dislodge such misgivings and focus on the task at hand.

"Thank you for seeing me on such short notice."

"Certainly. You said David was assaulted? When, where, how badly?"

To Clavel, he seemed genuinely surprised and concerned. He also did not look like an assailant. Marc Lafitte was medium in almost all respects: medium build, medium brown hair, medium-sized nose and eyes, middle age—fortyish. Completely forgettable. Of course, that would be an asset for a criminal. In any case, it was too early to write him off the list of possible suspects.

This was the tricky stage in an investigation. It was a balancing act. He needed to elicit as much information as possible while revealing as little as possible.

"Monsieur Barber, David, was found unconscious in his apartment this morning. He has been taken to the hospital. So far, we have few clues as to who or why he was attacked. We found your business card in the apartment and hope you can tell us something about him that might help explain why he was attacked."

"I'm not sure I can be of much help. It's just unbelievable. He was such a likable person—I can't imagine he had any enemies."

"You said something about investigative reporting?"

"Yes, he fancied himself as an investigative reporter unearthing major scandals and crimes. He always had big dreams."

"Always? How long have you know him?"

"We met in high school—Lycée Henri IV."

If this was meant to impress Clavel, it flopped—having attended himself, a fact he kept to himself and tried to forget.

"Have you kept in touch since then?"

"Sporadically over the years—emails and annual phone calls on our respective birthdays. After high school, David moved to the States for college to study journalism. After graduating, he took a job at the *Buffalo News*—a pretty good paper in Buffalo, New York—covering local politics. 'A stepping stone to bigger things,' he told me at the time. Apparently it did not work out that way, at least not as rapidly as he had hoped. In May, the twelfth—I remember because it's my daughter's birthday—he called announcing that he had come into some money, quit his job, and moved back to Paris, in his words 'in search of love and recognition.' He was born in France, and thanks to our *droit du sol* had French citizenship, which meant there were no restrictions on how long he could stay or where he could work. We agreed to meet for lunch the next day. When I asked him what all this was about—love and recognition—he said he was going to be a famous investigative reporter and marry his high-school sweetheart. It was typical David—a self-confident romantic."

"Go on," encouraged Clavel.

"I told him a bit about my life—how after studying art history at Beaux Arts I discovered that, while I had no creative talent, I had an eye for those that did and had put this to quite good use running this art gallery. But I digress—you're not interested in me. It was only as we ordered dessert that the real reason for David's having contacted me became clear. He had been looking for an apartment to buy for about seven months and had finally found his *'coup de coeur.'* It was love at first sight. The only hitch was that it was a *viager.* I told him not to buy it and tried to explain that, under a *viager* contract, the owner maintained the right to occupy the apartment until his death, and that in addition he, David, would have to pay a monthly 'fee' to the seller. I warned him that the owner could live for twenty more years. He said he knew all this but wondered if I knew anyone who had ever bought *en viager.* I had to admit I did not, but tried to persuade him that this was because my friends were too smart to do so. Well, he didn't listen, and that was lucky because less than a year later the owner died. I didn't hear from David again until Friday a week ago. He called to tell me that he had stumbled on a story that would make him that famous investigative reporter he was born to be. He said it involved works of art, and he wanted my opinion and advice. He didn't want to talk over the phone and offered to take me to lunch as a *quid pro quo*. I told him no *quid pro quo* was necessary but agreed to meet him for lunch this coming Monday—tomorrow. I was booked for an art fair in Chatou last week, not returning until this past Friday evening."

"If he had a story, I assume he would write it on a computer?"

"No doubt."

"What do you know about the story?"

"Only that it involved art works. He didn't say how many. If he wanted my advice, it must have had to do either with authentication or valuation—the only area in which I have any expertise."

"And no idea what the paintings were?"

"None. But since my expertise, such as it is, is in twentieth -century painting, a good guess would be that they were of that period."

"You mentioned a girlfriend."

"Yes, Micole Parnet. They were, as we used to say, 'an item' in high school. When he moved to the States, I assumed the flame had died out, but I guess I was wrong."

"Do you know where I can find her?"

"Yes, she works at the Musée Maillol."

"Well, thank you very much—you've been helpful. I may need to bother you again. And please take my card. If anything should occur to you that might be relevant, please contact me."

The Art Deco clock on the gallery wall, priced at €1,200, said 6:00 p.m. as Clavel rose to leave. There was no point in returning to his office that night, so he decided to walk home. At least he'd get a bit of the exercise to which he had planned to devote the day. And at that hour on a Sunday, he was unlikely to run into anyone he knew.

Place Beauvau was empty except for the guards posted in front of the Ministry of the Interior. So, too, was the rue Saint Honoré, except for the addition of a few tourists taking photos of the Elysée Palace. Passing Sotheby's auction house, he noticed that its next sale, on Thursday, was of Modern and Contemporary Art. He made a mental note that, if this case did in fact involve an art scam, Sotheby's experts might be of some help.

As he continued down the street past the high-fashion, high-price boutiques and toward the Madeleine, he decided to put the case out of his mind until tomorrow.

The steps of the Madeleine were in full bloom. He silently congratulated whoever was responsible for the installation of hundreds of flowerpots on the steps leading up to the famous church. Yes, Paris was a visually spectacular city, but it could still do with more flora, especially in this area of the *Grands Boulevards,* home to large department stores, cinemas, and five-star hotels.

At the Madeleine, he headed down boulevard des Capucines toward the Opéra Garnier. Glancing at the schedule for upcoming performances posted on the side of the opera house, he noticed that, the following week, they were doing *La Bayadère*, one of his favorite ballets. He'd have to try to get a ticket—maybe next Friday. His passion for ballet was one he carefully kept secret from his colleagues. French society may have evolved away from many male vs. female stereotypes, but within the police force, ballet remained stubbornly in the column of female activities—both for performers and for spectators. He had been of this view himself before his marriage, but Anne had changed that. She had been an aspiring dancer as a child but had abandoned her hopes as she grew into a Rubensesque woman. Her passion, however, remained and she slowly converted Clavel. On her first birthday after their wedding, she'd hinted that she would like to see *Swan Lake*. He would never forget her look of amusement when he produced one ticket. "I see Monsieur Policeman is too macho to see a ballet," she had said mockingly. After that, he always purchased two tickets and quickly became as passionate as she, although he tended to favor the more contemporary choreographers—*La Bayadère* being an exception.

Rather than go directly home, he took a short detour into the quartier Drouot. The auction house was of course closed, but he noted that it was open weekdays from 11:00 to 6:00, with extended hours on Thursday evenings. He pulled out his notebook —his staff called it his "guide"—and made a note to send Claire to gather information about the auction.

Passing the taxi stand where his day had begun and looking up the gently sloping rue des Martyrs, Clavel suddenly felt tired. And hungry. He often said cooking was his favorite form of relaxation, but not that night. Chez Plum's excellent spit-roasted chicken and accompanying potatoes and green beans offered a perfect solution. He disliked eating out alone so he ordered it to go. He considered chicken to be the gods' gift to cooks. It leant itself to so many varied preparations. He considered himself rather an accomplished cook but had never mastered a simple roast chicken. *Poulet à l'estragon* was his specialty, the dish he inevitably served to guests. With heavy cream and fresh tarragon, you couldn't go wrong.

As he turned the corner onto rue Condorcet, it began to rain. He quickened his pace and reached his front door damp but not soaked. After changing into sweatpants and a T-shirt, he turned on the radio and, to the sounds of Thelonius Monk, sat down to enjoy his dinner and think over his day.

It certainly hadn't been the Sunday he had planned. But he wasn't sorry. This Barber case promised to be among the more intriguing he had handled in a while. And, as his ex-wife had often said, nothing gave him as much joy as an intricate criminal investigation.

CHAPTER 4

C LAVEL WAS GLAD TO SEE THAT, true to form, his secretary, Mme Pinan, was already at her desk when he arrived in the office at 7:45 Monday morning. As with all his cases, the first thing he wanted to do was describe the case to her. Keeping her in the loop was a cardinal rule in the office. Over the years, she had helped him solve many a case, suggesting that so-and-so had been lying, or that he really ought to talk to X. She claimed her intuition came from reading whodunits. He found that hard to believe, given how silly most such books were, but no matter.

After listening silently to Clavel's description of what he had learned thus far, Mme Pinan looked up and said, "You need to talk to Olivier."

Having always found it helpful to observe people in their everyday environment, Clavel took his hat and headed to Peggy Huyn, the high-fashion design shop on rue Coëtlogon where Mme Corez had said Olivier worked. He decided to pose as a rich husband in search of a present for his wife. Hiding one's true identity while investigating cases was discouraged in the department but it was an approach favored by Clavel.

As with many such micro-establishments, the door was locked. The lights were on, so he rang the bell. After several minutes, a young woman appeared from the back room and let him in. She was tall and willowy, with shoulder-length black hair held back by a silver headband. Her leopard skin-patterned pants clung to her like skin.

"May I help you?" she asked with an insincere smile.

Looking around, Clavel noticed a number of colorful bags on display. "I'm looking for a large leather handbag for my wife," he said, thinking the number of choices would provide an opportunity to linger. He wasn't sure how he would trigger the appearance of Olivier. He needn't have worried. Before the woman could reply, a modishly dressed young man appeared from the back.

"Olivier, would you please help this gentleman. He's looking for a handbag for his wife. I'll leave you in Olivier's hands. Bags are his area of expertise," she said, returning to what Clavel assumed was the workshop.

Olivier could have walked straight off the pages of a high-fashion magazine. Swarthy, with large, almond-shaped jet black eyes and coiffed thick, curly black hair, he was dressed in made-to-measure dark gray slacks that accentuated his admirable build, and a dark red cashmere sweater with a silk cravat knotted at the V- shaped neck.

"What sort of bag are you looking for?"

"Something for traveling—lightweight with many compartments."

"The lightest we have is this one," Oliver said, taking a bag off the display case. "It's specifically designed for travel. There is a pocket for passport and documents, two pockets for different currencies, and both a handle and a shoulder strap."

"Yes, this might do," said Clavel after carefully examining the bag. "Does it come in other colors? She is not fond of black."

"At the moment we only have it in black but we can make one for you in any of these colors," replied Olivier pulling out a book of leather samples.

Perfect, thought Clavel. He would have an excuse for a subsequent visit.

"How long would it take?"

"I could have it for you in five or six days."

"And the price would be the same as the bag on display?"

"Yes. We'd require a deposit of 150 euros, half the price."

Clavel hoped the department would see this as a justifiable expense. A €300 women's handbag was hardly within his personal budget.

"Fine. I assume you accept credit cards."

"Of course," smiled Olivier, clearly glad to have such an easy sale.

As he waited for the transaction to clear, Clavel casually looked over the other items on sale—leather bags, wallets, agenda books and glasses' cases all at ridiculously high prices.

"Who designs your products?" Clavel asked.

"I design the bags. The other items are designed by my colleagues."

"You're very talented. I assume you design for other companies as well?" asked Clavel, hoping flattery would get him somewhere.

"No. This is just a short-term occupation. I don't plan to be designing handbags for too much longer, for anyone."

"Well, I'm glad I discovered you before you move on. I'll be back next week."

Walking back toward the quai des Orfèvres, Clavel went over what had he learned for his extravagant purchase. Olivier was an extremely seductive, arrogant young man with, judging by his clothes, expensive taste. Tastes which he probably could not afford on his income as a designer of handbags for a small boutique, especially if his life-style was consistent with his wardrobe. Is that why he wanted to "move on"? Certainly, stealing valuable art offered the possibility of greater wealth. But what was his life-style? There was one way to find out. He stopped and pulled out his cell phone.

"Claire?"

"Yes, *chef*."

"Drop whatever you're doing and come to nine rue Coëtlogon in the sixth. I want you to tail someone for the Barber case. Dress in civilian clothes."

Claire was the perfect tail for Olivier—a young, attractive woman. If she attracted Olivier's attention, it wouldn't be because he suspected her of being a cop.

CHAPTER 5

C LAVEL HAD BEEN SKEPTICAL when Claire Simon was assigned to his team of inspectors. She was far from the usual hire. She was a graduate of the University of Geneva in Switzerland, with a degree in art history, who had entered the police academy only after working at the Corbier auction house in Paris. He remembered thinking at the time that the move to diversify the force was getting out of hand. He had even asked his boss to reconsider. It wasn't long before he was glad his request had been denied. Claire was one of the hardest-working, most intelligent investigators on his staff. And her background turned out to be an asset, not a liability.

After graduation, Claire had become a *stagiaire*—a low-paid internship considered a right of passage in many professions—at Corbier in its modern and contemporary art department.

"After a year, I was hired on a CDI—*contrat de durée indéterminée*—contract. Meaning I had a job for life, and that is what I intended it to be," Claire had told Clavel on one of the many long evenings they had spent in the car, tailing a suspect.

"Then, in my third year, my department was enmeshed in a messy legal battle over the sale of a Roy Lichtenstein. An American collector had purchased the work for thirty million dollars at Corbier's spring auction, outbidding four others. Within a month, he was back demanding a refund, claiming the work was a fake. He said that his wife did not like the work—saying its colors clashed with the rest of her décor." Claire laughed, remembering the snobbish distain this explanation had evoked among Corbier's staff. "When he had tried to resell it, he was told it was a fake. A battle of the experts followed. After eighteen months, a settlement was reached. Corbier offered to refund the purchase price while maintaining that the work was a genuine Lichtenstein. In the view of the management, a settlement was necessary if they were to continue to attract wealthy buyers. They were probably correct— who would spend millions if they could not rely on the accuracy of the experts' evaluation of a work? 'Satisfaction or your money back' is as an effective sales pitch for art as for stereos.

"Unfortunately, this particular buyer refused to settle and sued the company. His lawyers ultimately were able to prove that Corbier's owners occasionally paid outside 'experts' to authenticate fakes and provide certificates of authenticity. They tended to sell the fakes to rich clients, often Americans who didn't know or care about art but simply wanted to own works by big-name artists. The buyers were provided with erroneous attributions, and everyone was happy—until a buyer decided to resell and found he had a fake. This didn't happen often, and when it did the company quickly settled in order not to attract attention. It had worked beautifully for over a decade."

"But you resigned almost immediately, so I gather you suspected the client had a good case?" asked Clavel.

"No, I resigned because I found I was more interested in exposing those who provided false authentications than in doing the authenticating. As a new hire, I was tasked to help the experts gather evidence that works were authentic and were obtained legally by the seller. Most of the works Corbier's sold were so-called 'clean,' just not all of them. I guess I was naïve, but I had no idea how difficult it is to verify a painting's provenance and authenticity. Or how important. The number of fakes and stolen works sold by the world's top galleries and action houses is humongous. Technology has made forgery incredibly easy and difficult to detect. And with the price of certain artists in the stratosphere, incredibly lucrative. And it turns out many collectors are willing to ignore doubts about authenticity to get hold of a coveted work."

"So you decided to join the crusade to cleanse the market?" asked Clavel with a twinkle in his eye.

"You could put it that way," laughed Claire. "I guess I do care that the unchecked sale of fakes and stolen works will delegitimize the entire field. But mostly I just find it fascinating to try to detect the scams."

"A selfish motive for noble work," nodded Clavel approvingly.

From day one, he and Claire had understood each other and this type of banter was common.

Given her background in the art market, it was obvious to Clavel that Claire had to be part of the Barber case team. As yet, there was no proof, but Clavel was convinced that the break-in and assault were related to David's reported suspicions about an art scam.

CHAPTER 6

HAVING BRIEFED CLAIRE on the little he knew about Olivier and what he wanted her to find out, Clavel headed to the Musée Maillol. He had never been there and was pleased to have a reason to do so.

"Bonjour—is Madame Parnet here?" he inquired of the elderly woman selling tickets.

"What is it you want? Perhaps I can help you," she replied, eyeing him skeptically.

"It's a private matter," Clavel answered, hoping to avoid revealing his identity.

"Perhaps then you should contact her after work hours."

My luck, a self-important, insignificant bureaucrat, thought Clavel as he pulled out his badge.

"Oh, excuse me, Commissaire," said the now-smiling woman. "I'll call her right away."

Before he could replace his badge, a young woman emerged from the door just behind the ticket desk. She was what Clavel assumed would be called "petite"—no more than five feet tall and extremely thin. She was dressed entirely in black—black high heels, tight black pants, a loose black sweater, and long, dangling black-and-gold earrings. Her short black hair completed the ensemble. Study in black, thought Clavel, clearly under the influence of the museum setting.

"Micole, this is Commissaire Clavel. He wants to speak with you."

"Thank you, Delphine."

"Please," said Micole, opening the door from which she had emerged into a small office.

"Won't you sit down," she said, pointing to one of two desk chairs. "We can speak privately here. I assume you have come about David," she said, her voice cracking and tears coming to her eyes. "I'm sorry," she said, wiping the eyes and trying to smile. "It's all so horrid and inexplicable. And I feel it's my fault. He never would have come to Paris were it not for me."

"Are you old friends?"

"We met at the Lycée and became very close. But not close enough to keep him in Paris," she said with a wistful smile. "He was set on going to a U.S. university, which he was convinced were the best in the world. He promised he'd come back, but I didn't believe him."

"But he did," interjected Clavel, "and thanks to you."

"Yes. He had come into money and was dissatisfied with his career as a journalist. I encouraged him to come back, even suggesting he might help me in my new position here at Musée Maillol. In high school he had been interested in art and had even considered getting a Ph.D. in art history but had opted for journalism instead."

"And did he? Help you, that is?"

"Initially, yes, helping me with some research I was doing. But then, soon after he moved into his new apartment, he became totally obsessed with investigating what he said was a major story. He wouldn't tell me anything more until he had more evidence."

"Do you know if David told anyone else about his suspicion? People who might want to silence him?"

"I doubt it. He told me not to tell anyone—not that I had anything to tell."

"Did he have any enemies, anyone who would wish him ill?"

"Oh, no. Everyone liked David. It was impossible not to."

"Did he have anything of value, anything someone would want to steal?"

"Not that I know of. He had inherited a good deal of money, as I said, but I'm sure he didn't keep cash at home and, as far as I know, he hadn't purchased anything other than basic furniture since he arrived."

Clavel nodded. This was all consistent with what he knew already. He thanked her for her time and left his card, urging her to call if anything occurred to her that might help in the investigation.

CHAPTER 7

THE NEXT DAY, JUST AS CLAVEL ARRIVED in his office, the phone rang. "Commissaire Clavel?"

"Speaking."

"This is Micole Parnet, David's friend. I just remembered some things—I'm sure they aren't important, but you said to call."

"Yes?" replied Clavel. "But first let me tell you the good news. David has regained consciousness, and the doctors say he's out of danger."

"Oh, that's terrific. Can I visit him?"

"Better to wait. I'm told he has lost his memory. He doesn't even remember his name or anything about his past. He wouldn't recognize you."

"But I'd recognize him," she pleaded.

"No, I'm afraid the doctors won't allow any visits for the moment. Not even of the police. I'll let you know the minute visits are allowed. Now, tell me why you called."

"Yes, well, I told you David didn't tell me anything about his suspicions, which is true, but he did ask me if I knew any lawyers who specialized in art law. I suggested he might want to talk to lawyers at Desrobert—they specialize in crimes involving art. They've contacted me several times to ask whether we had a particular painting in our collection."

"Did they ever say why they wanted to know?"

"No. Of course, I asked, but they said they weren't at liberty to tell me."

"Do you know if David contacted them?"

"I'm sorry, I don't."

"Do you mind if I check with them myself?"

"Of course not. And I suppose you would do so even if I did object," she said with an engaging laugh.

"Yes, I suppose I would. Was there anything else?"

"Well, I don't mean to accuse anyone," she began hesitantly.

"Of course not. Please go on."

"Well, the day after the owner, Pierre, died, David asked me to meet him at the apartment. He said he wanted me to look at the art and tell him if there was anything I thought he should bid on at the auction. I walked up and, just as I was approaching the landing, I saw Dr. Lotan standing in front of David's door. At the time, I had the impression he was pulling the door shut. He seemed startled and displeased at seeing me. When I asked if I could help him, he said no and mumbled something about having hoped David was in to discuss something about an upcoming meeting of the tenants' association. I told him David would be arriving any minute. He said he couldn't wait and would come back another time. He seemed in a hurry to leave."

"Think back and describe Lotan to me."

"Describe? I'm sure it was he. I met him when David and I went to look at the apartment for the first time. We got there early and were waiting outside for the agent when he came out. He asked if he could help us, as if he thought we were up to no good. Before we could answer, the agent arrived and introduced us."

"Actually, I was not questioning whether it was the doctor. I just want you to describe him on that occasion. For example, was he wearing a coat and hat, as if he had just come in or was going out?"

"Let me think," said Micole, closing her eyes as if to recapture the moment. "He was carrying a coat over his arm but not wearing a hat. It was raining, and I don't recall his having an umbrella, so I doubt he was going out. Of course, he could have had an umbrella on his arm under the coat."

"Did you mention this to David?"

"Yes, but he just shrugged it off, saying that, if it was important, the doctor would come back. He was sure I had imagined that the doctor was coming out of the apartment. Do you think it's important? Could the doctor have something to do with the break-in?"

"It's too early to know what role, if any, he played, but all information is important at this stage in the investigation. By the way, did you suggest David bid on any of the art?"

"No, in fact I told him I didn't like anything, but that, if he wanted a souvenir of Pierre, he should just be sure not to overpay."

CHAPTER 8

HANGING UP THE PHONE, Clavel leaned back, closed his eyes, and thought about the doctor. Admittedly, he didn't like him, had found him an arrogant snob. But that didn't make him a criminal. And yet he did suspect him. Why? Suddenly he opened his eyes and reached for the crime scene investigators' report. He had been so intrigued by Lafitte's business card and the computer cord that he hadn't focused on the rest of the report. Flipping through the pages, he found what he was looking for. The team had found a small quantity of loose tobacco under an overturned table in the living room. Forensics had identified it as pipe tobacco. That explained the odor he had detected on his initial visit.

"Jean-Paul, Clavel here. I'm reading your team's report on the Barber crime scene. It says they found pipe tobacco. Can you be more precise?"

"It isn't a type we recognize. It must be a rare variety."

"I need you to identify the tobacco. Contact an outside expert if you need to. It could be important."

How had pipe tobacco, rare pipe tobacco, come to be in the apartment? Clavel wondered. Micole had said David didn't smoke, so the source had to have been a visitor. Clavel didn't imagine many of David's guests smoked pipes. Few people did. Almost certainly not the vandals. One person who did, however, was Lotan.

It was clear a visit to the doctor was in order. Less clear was how to approach him. A quick phone call settled the issue. Mme Corez eagerly agreed to arrange a meeting with Lotan for that evening.

Clavel brought a bottle of expensive wine for Lotan and a bouquet of flowers for Mme Corez. The gifts were meant to signal that Clavel was not there on official police business.

Seemingly they did so. Lotan welcomed Clavel with a smile and complimented him on his choice of wine.

"I only wish I knew as much about art as I do wine," joked Clavel.

"Ah, yes, I understand you want some advice about a possible purchase," replied Lotan, nodding toward Mme Corez.

"Yes. I have a collection of photographs that has proven to be a rather good investment. I was thinking it might be a good idea to invest in some paintings as well, and I was hoping you might be able to provide me some advice."

"Do you have particular items in mind?"

"No, no particular paintings, but I would be most interested in early twentieth-century works. They might be out of my price range, but I like Charmy, Laubser, and Por,"replied Clavel, listing some lesser-known artists Claire had told him were associated with the Fauve movement.

"Hm. Well, those artists are all what are referred to as Fauves and are very much in demand at the moment. They won't come cheaply, but they are certainly available."

"Where would you suggest I look?" asked Clavel, taking out his pen and notebook to record the advice.

"There are several galleries that specialize in the period,. and I'd also talk to the major auction houses—Sotheby's, Christie's, Artcurial. They often arrange what are called 'private sales' and may well have clients interested in selling."

The doctor provided the names of a half-dozen galleries without indicating a preference.

"Thank you. I'll start my search this weekend," said Clavel, closing his notebook and picking up his glass of wine.

"Before you buy anything, I think you should check back with George, don't you agree?" said Mme Corez, putting her hand on the doctor's arm.

"Yes, of course. I'd be happy to give my opinion."

Clavel doubted he would have been so accommodating in the absence of Mme Corez and decided to make the most of her presence.

"Thank you both. May I ask your opinion on another matter?"

"Certainly," replied the doctor somewhat hesitantly.

"It's about tobacco, pipe tobacco," said Clavel, pointing to the doctor's pipe collection.

"Tobacco?" chuckled the doctor. "I'm not an expert. I just enjoy an occasional smoke."

"Oh, but you are. You were just telling me about the new shop you had discovered that had such a variety of exotic blends," interrupted Mme Corez.

"Would you let me in on the discovery?" asked Clavel with a slight laugh and a wink at Mme Corez. He wanted to keep it light-hearted lest the doctor guess his real motive in asking.

"Here, tell them I sent you—maybe I'll get a kickback," said the doctor, laughing and handing Clavel the shop's business card.

Heading home, Clavel felt very pleased with himself. He had learned far more than he had anticipated.

CHAPTER 9

D RESSED IN BEIGE PANTS and a bright red jacket, Claire looked like anything but a police officer. Unfortunately, the rue Coëtlogon offered few places where a person, even a civilian, could hang around without looking conspicuous. Peggy Huyn was the only shop other than the fruit and vegetable stand on the corner, and there was just so long you could survey a fruit display. After having done so for several minutes, Claire began strolling down the block, looking frequently at her watch as if she were waiting for someone. Just as she was about to return to fruit-gazing, a man matching the description Clavel had given her of Olivier walked out of Peggy Huyn. She followed him as he hurried toward the place Saint Germain, down rue Bonaparte, and entered the bistro Pré aux Clercs on the corner of rue Jacob. She waited a few minutes and entered herself. Looking around, she saw him seated in back in the company of another, equally elegant young man. The table next to theirs was empty, and hopefully not reserved.

"A table in the back, please," she told the waiter, pointing to one in question.

"That table is for two. I can seat you here by the window," he said, pointing to a table from which she would not be able to observe, and hopefully overhear, her prey.

"We will be two—my friend should be arriving shortly."

The waiter looked skeptical but seated her and left her to study the menu, and to listen to her neighbors' conversation, which for a good ten minutes focused on the merits of various dishes on that menu. Olivier ultimately chose the duck breast and his companion the veal with morels. Both expressed satisfaction with their choice.

The first non-culinary words Claire caught were Olivier's: "I want a hundred thousand. I trusted you, and you lied. Pay, or I talk."

"Your accusation is insulting and absurd."

"You're wrong, Jacques, I *do* have proof, and I'll use it."

Claire made a mental note—*Jacques.*

"Go ahead, you'll just make a fool of yourself," said Jacques, signaling the waiter for the bill.

"I'll give you a week. And thanks for lunch," said Olivier, nodding to him, and walked out.

The waiter was nowhere to be seen, so Claire left a twenty-euro bill on the table, far more than the cost of her salade niçoise, and followed him.

After buying some cigarettes, Olivier returned to Peggy Huyn. It was only 3:00 p.m. The boutique closed at 6:00. If she followed her instructions to the letter, she would wait on the street until Olivier came back out, which could be three hours. But she had not risen in the ranks by blindly following orders. In fact, Clavel more than once had complemented her on "using her brain" and taking initiative.

And her brain told her Jacques was an important player, and that she needed more than a first name. She couldn't very well ask Olivier, but she could ask the waiter. He probably wouldn't know much about him, as she doubted Jacques was the sort to befriend a waiter, but he should be able at least to tell her Jacques' last name, since he had paid the bill, hopefully with a credit card. Whether he would tell her was another question.

The place was still busy, and it took her a moment to spot her waiter. He noticed her at the same time.

"Come back for your change?"

"No, I'm terribly sorry to have rushed off, but I had an emergency call from my office."

"Hm," said the waiter, clearly not believing a word of it.

"Yes, and I'm so embarrassed to have to ask you this," she said with her best imitation of a scatterbrained flirt. "But I was speaking to two gentlemen at the table next to mine and I promised to call them—well, call Jacques, the one with the mustache—with some information about an upcoming art show. The problem is I forgot to get his contact information. I was hoping you might know them."

"Monsieur Allard. Sure, I know him, he comes here often, but I don't have any contact information. If you leave me your number, I'll give it to him next time I see him, and he can call you. If he wants to, that is."

"Oh, I'm sure he'd want to," she giggled, "but the show is this evening, and I don't suppose he'll be back again today."

"No, probably not," said the waiter with a smile, indicating he wasn't falling for this story either.

"That is too bad, but thank you anyway," said Claire, hoping the waiter would have forgotten this conversation before he saw Allard again.

Back at the fruit stand, Claire called headquarters to brief Clavel. He agreed to ask Luc to see what he could find out about a Jacques Allard.

CHAPTER 10

WHILE CLAIRE WAS EAVESDROPPING on Olivier and Jacques, across the Atlantic in Buffalo, New York, Prof. Jersey was preparing a lecture for his class on investigative journalism at SUNY Buffalo. The topic for the next day's class was *Protecting Sources: The Law and Ethics.* It was a topic he enjoyed because it usually led to a heated debate among the students, pitting those who thought journalists should reveal the identity of their sources if asked to do so by a court and those who would go to jail rather than do so. He was jotting down arguments on both sides of the debate when he stopped and reached for the trashcan.

It hadn't hit him at first. A few lines in the *Buffalo News*. He fished the paper out of the can to check his recollection. Yes, there it was.

Assault in Paris, screamed the headline. "David Barber, a former *Buffalo News* reporter, was found brutally beaten in his apartment in Paris's prestigious Sixth arrondissement. He remains in a local hospital. The apartment had been ransacked.

No arrests have been made. The police remain closed-mouthed about the investigation." That was it. Five factual sentences.

He picked up the phone. "Joe, this is Jersey."

"Jersey! What a surprise. To what do I owe the honor?"

"I just noticed the Barber story, if you can call the five lines a story. Is that really all you know?"

"It's all the facts, yes. You know we don't print rumors and speculation."

"Right. Is anyone on your staff following the story, looking for more?"

"No. We'll monitor the local French press, but we don't have the staff to do our own reporting."

"So your source is the French press?"

"Come on, Jersey, what do you expect us to do, send a team to Paris to cover every break-in?"

"No, but this isn't just any break-in. David was a reporter for you, for god's sake. And he was viciously assaulted. David's the story."

"True, but as you know, he resigned, and he has no continuing connection to Buffalo. Anyway, why are you so interested?"

"David was a student of mine, and one with great potential, which, incidentally, you failed to recognize."

"You bet we didn't recognize it. His work was mediocre at best. Of course I'm sorry he's been hurt, but it really isn't newsworthy."

"Would it be newsworthy if I told you I had some idea of why he was assaulted?"

". . .Do you?"

"I think so, yes. I was hoping your reporters might have information that would confirm my suspicions."

"As I said, they don't. Why don't you come by, tell me what you have, and maybe we can put someone on it."

"Thanks. When suits you?"

"It's ten now. Why don't you come around noon? I'll spring for lunch."

"Generous of you! I'll be there. *À bientôt.*"

"And the man speaks French. I'm duly impressed," Joe chuckled.

He had two hours. If he left now, he'd have time to stop at the library on the way. Hopefully, they had a travel book on Paris.

He arrived right on time at the *Buffalo News* offices burdened by two books and printouts of his email correspondence with David.

Joe suggested they go to the deli around the corner from the paper. Jersey was more than happy to agree—it offered the best pastrami on rye outside New York City. And the less-than-efficient service meant he'd have plenty of time to make his case.

The place was packed and noisy. Any serious discussion seemed out of the question. As Jersey was about to suggest going elsewhere, a waiter scurried up and ushered them to a private booth in the back.

"Journalist privilege," smiled Joe.

"I think I object, but not today," winked Jersey.

"What'll it be, Joe?" asked the waiter, who clearly knew the routine—order quickly and leave them alone.

"I'll have pastrami on rye with a diet root beer," said Joe.

"Make that two, but a non-diet RB for me," said Jersey, already pulling his documents out of his backpack.

"OK, what do you have?" asked Joe.

"Aren't you going to ask how my book is coming along?" smiled Jersey.

"Nope, this is business, and anyhow, it's risky to ask about books."

"Not in this case. The book is almost finished."

"Great. Now, what do you have to merit our interest in Barber?"

"As you know, David was a student of mine, one of the very few who had an interest in investigative reporting."

"Your passion."

"Yes, I think our country would be better off if more journalists spent time deeply investigating topics and less trying to get a byline per day. Unfortunately, few young people today seem to have the patience to spend weeks or even years researching a story, and too many papers prioritize being first with a scoop."

"Yeah, the *Buffalo News* included," interrupted Joe.

"Absolutely. But we've discussed that before. I raise it now just to explain why I kept up with David after he graduated. I wanted to encourage him to stick to his ambition. Frankly, I was disappointed when he joined your paper and glad when he quit."

"Sentiments I share," winked Joe.

"Right. Anyway, when he told me he was going to Paris, I told him I hoped he was not giving up journalism, and he assured me he was not. He said that, thanks to his inheritance, he no longer needed to have a regular job with a paper and planned to do 'reporting, through one's own initiative and work product, on matters of importance to readers'—quoting Professor Steve Weinberg's definition of investigative journalism. I wished him luck, and we agreed to keep in touch, and did."

"On what 'matter of importance to readers' did he plan to report?" asked Joe in a mocking tone.

"He didn't say, but I know he was interested in white-collar crime."

Jersey handed Joe copies of several emails.

"As you'll see in these emails, he thought he finally had a story that would launch his career as an investigative journalist. The fact that he was attacked just days after sending that email seems to justify at least the suspicion that the two are related."

"And you think also justifies our doing some investigative reporting of our own?"

"In a word, yes."

"I can't disagree, but I'm not sure we have the staff. You know how stretched we are these days. Our budget is very tight."

"If you assign one reporter, I'll provide four students from my investigative reporting class to help with the research."

"Give me a day or so to discuss this with the powers-that-be. Can you let me have these?" asked Joe, tapping the emails.

"Of course. And, Joe, thanks. I really appreciate it, and I don't think you'll regret it. My sixth sense tells me there is something here, something big."

"I'll do my best but make no promises."

"You could tell the big guys it might finally win them a Pulitzer that isn't for editorial cartooning," said Jersey with a smile.

"Right," replied Joe, shaking his head and wondering why Jersey so enjoyed mocking the paper.

CHAPTER 11

"CHEF," SAID LUC, STICKING HIS HEAD around the open door into Clavel's office.

"Come in, come in."

"I have the information you requested on Jacques Allard," he said, pulling out his notebook. "He was born in Lyon, moved to Paris five years ago to attend l'École des Beaux Arts. According to the school's records, right after graduating he took a job at the Danine gallery on the rue de Seine. Their records only cover the first position after graduation, unless of course the student rises to fame and glory. Madame Danine, the owner of the gallery, says she engaged Jacques on a one-year contract with the understanding that, if it worked out, she would give him a CDI, a contract of indeterminate duration, i.e., permanent. It didn't—didn't work out, that is, and she let him go after a year. She has no idea where he went after that, and didn't seem interested." Luc closed his notebook and waited.

Clavel appreciated Luc's loyalty and effort but often won-

dered at his intelligence. He always left out obviously important information.

"Did you ask her why it didn't 'work out,' as you put it?"

"No, she simply said he was not satisfactory."

"I wish you'd pressed her on that. It would be useful to
know, give us an idea about his character. I gather you didn't
talk to anyone at the school who might have known him, a
professor, say?"

"No. Do you want me to go back?"

"No, that's fine for now," sighed Clavel. "But I want you
to pay a visit to Olivier Novochkin. He works at a boutique
on rue Coëtlogon called Peggy Huyn. See what you can find
out about his current economic situation."

Clavel didn't think Luc was likely to uncover any useful
information, but Olivier would certainly expect a visit by the
police and the last thing he wanted was for him to suspect
Claire or himself. Hopefully after Luc's inept questioning, Olivier would feel safe and let down his guard.

CHAPTER 12

RETURNING TO RUE COËTLOGON, Claire was beginning to regret her choice of shoes. High heels were ill-suited for this stakeout. Rather than stare at fruit, she pulled out her cell phone and strolled up and down the street pretending to concentrate on an important conversation. She was relieved to see a few others doing the same. At 6:00 sharp, Olivier came out. Someone who worked to the clock, she thought. Someone who had plans other than a career at Peggy Huyn. What those plans were she hoped to discover. She followed him to the Métro at Sèvres-Babylone. The station was crowded as always at that hour so she was able to follow him onto the train without being noticed. Following him as he got off the train at the Cardinale Lemoine station and walked down the street to number 34 was just as easy. She checked the mailboxes—O. Novochkin, 5th floor.

"*Chef*, Claire here. I'm on the rue Cardinale Lemoine, next to the Hôtel le Brun. Olivier just went inside an apartment building . There's a mailbox for O. Novochkin, so I assume it's his residence. What do I do now? I can't very well ring the bell and invite myself in."

"You could. He'd probably be pleased, but I don't recommend it," Clavel laughed.

"Do you want me to wait and see if he goes back out?"

"Yes, but only for an hour. If he hasn't come out by eight, go home."

"Deal. I'll see you in the office in the morning."

It was 7:00. Fortunately, there was a small Afghan restaurant across the street, *Kootchi* by name. She took a seat at a table by a window from which she could see the apartment building.

She glanced quickly at the menu, keeping one eye on the apartment. She was starved. A salade niçoise was meager sustenance for hours pacing up and down the street, in high heels.

"A chicken kebab and a Perrier" she told the waiter before he escaped to serve other clients, "and the check, please." She didn't want to have to wait for it if Olivier happened to appear.

She needn't have worried. It was just past 8:00 when she finished what turned out to be a surprisingly good kebab—neither dry nor greasy—and no sign of Olivier. Her instincts told her to wait for another twenty minutes. If a club or other nocturnal entertainment were on his agenda, he probably wouldn't head out until at least 8:30. Moreover, she was still hungry.

She signaled he waiter and ordered an espresso and an apricot tart.

"And another check?"

"And another check," she said in a cheerful voice, pretending not to have noticed his surly tone.

She had just finished the tart when she saw Olivier come out and wave for a taxi.

Gulping down her coffee, she rushed out, jostling an elderly woman who made her opinion of young people clear to everyone in the restaurant.

To her relief, Oliver was still standing at the curb with his arm in the air. She did an imitation and was rewarded almost immediately as a taxi rounded the corner and stopped in front of her.

"Follow the taxi that picks up the man across the street."

"I can't idle here."

"You don't have to, he's being picked up."

Fortunately, traffic was light, and the two cabs proceeded as one down the boulevard Saint-Germain, across the Pont de Sully through the place de la Bastille, down boulevard Richard Lenoir to rue du Faubourg Saint-Denis. Once dominated by prostitutes, the area was now home to trendy clubs and bars. Olivier's cab pulled up in front of Chez Jeannette. Claire's stopped just behind him.

"Here?" asked the driver.

"Yes, thank you." Claire waited to get out, fiddling with her wallet until she saw Olivier enter the club.

He was shown a seat at a small table near the stage. Claire was glad to see the place was packed and that there were only three seats left near the stage.

"A seat by the stage," she said, pointing to the seat closest to Olivier. She smiled thinking how she had used a similar maneuver at the Pré aux Clercs at lunch. She hoped Olivier hadn't noticed her, or didn't remember.

So far so good, she thought as she was shown her chosen seat. She quickly pulled the pins out of her chignon, letting her wavy auburn hair fall loosely on her shoulders in a hairstyle more appropriate to the setting and different from the one she had at lunchtime.

After ordering a glass of white wine, which she didn't plan to drink, she pulled out a cigarette, which she didn't plan to smoke. Ordering a drink was a requirement, as was staying sober, and cigarettes were an invaluable prop in her chosen role as *femme fatale*.

"Do you have a light?" she asked, leaning toward Olivier.

"Of course," he said, and eyed her approvingly.

"Have we met before?" he asked.

Damn, she thought, he recognizes me from this afternoon.

"I don't think so. I'd remember you if we had," she replied, smiling and looking him directly in the eyes in a sign of utmost confidence.

"Well, I'm glad we met now," he said, pulling his chair closer to hers.

He was a very attractive man, and knew it: the type that would expect women to say "yes." This made Claire's job easy. She was sure she had only to wait and he would ask her to come home with him. The problem would come when they got there. She wasn't sure how resistant she could be without killing any chance of seeing him again. And seeing him again, and again, was going to be necessary. From what Clavel had told her, she assumed Olivier was a key suspect—and someone who had plenty of useful information that he did not want the police to have.

Within half an hour, Claire was in a taxi with Olivier, headed back to his apartment. Olivier was already tipsy and Claire figured that, with a bit of encouragement, he would soon be drunk. If she was lucky, he was the type that became talkative and then fall asleep. If not, and he turned out to be someone who became aggressive under the influence, she knew how to defend herself.

"Time for some champagne," Olivier announced as he turned on the lights, revealing a stunning, modish, expensively furnished apartment that bore the unmistakable imprint of its occupant. There could be no doubt that the owner and interior designer were one and the same. The arrangement of the furniture was striking. The low glass-top tables, which normally would be placed next to a chair or canapé sofa, were instead lined up under the two large windows giving onto the square across the street. On them were arranged a dozen colorfully decorated black lacquer boxes which Claire guessed were from Russia. The black leather canapé was placed against the opposite wall facing the line of tables. Four matching easy chairs occupied the four corners of the room. Next to each chair was a revolving book case and a tall pedestal reading lamp. One of the bookcases was full of auction catalogues. The others housed a mixture of art history books and popular fiction. The walls were covered with photographs of jazz musicians. There was also a lithograph by Gen Paul of a jazz quartet. He was an artist she adored but could not afford.

"Hungry?" came a voice from the kitchen.

"No," replied Claire, although she was, calculating that food might sober him up.

"*Et voilà*," said Olivier, bowing slightly as he handed her a cut glass champagne flute.

She smiled in reply and took a sip. It was excellent, not a budget brand.

As she knew he would, Olivier seated himself on the sofa.

"Join me, please," he said, tapping the place next to him— again as predicted.

Ignoring the invitation, she raised her glass and took a sip.

"Are you a photographer?" she asked, looking around at the walls.

"No. I tried but wasn't very good."

"So you collect?"

"I guess you could say that. How about you? Let me guess—a model?"

Claire had heard that line too often to be flattered, but she played along. "Nice of you to think so, but no, just a secretary," a cover she had used before. Men seemed to take for granted that a secretary would find them attractive and accede to their desires. It never crossed their minds that a secretary would have ulterior motives for seeking their company—an attitude she found offensive, albeit useful.

"I bet you play an instrument," she said, trying to move the conversation back to him.

"Wrong again," he laughed.

"Just a rich playboy, then?" she said with her most engaging smile.

"Bingo."

"This is excellent," she said raising her glass.

"More?"

"Yes, just a bit." Her glass was still three-fourths full but his was empty, and as she predicted, he filled both.

"Do you go to Jeannette's often?" Claire asked.

"There, and other places in the area."

"Which is your favorite? I only know Jeannette's."

"It's good, but I prefer New Morning."

"I'll have to give it a try."

"How about Saturday?" asked Olivier with a smile. Exactly the response Claire had been hoping for.

She smiled and stared at him for a minute before responding, "Sure. I'll meet you there. And now I should be off," she said, rising and placing her half-full glass on the table. He clearly wasn't going to reveal much about himself tonight.

"It's still early, and you haven't finished your champagne," said Olivier, taking the glass in one hand and putting his other arm around her shoulders.

She gently removed the arm, gave him a quick kiss on the cheek and headed toward the door.

He gently took her hand and kissed it.

A true romantic, reflected Claire. She'd have to be careful or she'd fall for him.

CHAPTER 13

Ask Claire to see me when she comes in," Clavel instructed Mme Pinan.

"She's waiting in your office."

"Thank you," replied Clavel, glancing at his watch. It was only 8:00 a.m.

"Exciting evening?" he asked, dropping into the chair behind his desk, when Claire entered.

"Interesting," she said, and smiled .

"Good work," said Clavel after listening to Claire's amusing rendition of her evening. "Hopefully. you can find out more about his activities and source of revenue next Saturday."

"What do you suspect?"

"Nothing in particular, but from what you say he seems to be living beyond whatever means he is earning from designing handbags."

"You think he has additional revenue, and that it's related to the Barber case?"

"Yes. He may be perfectly innocent. But I doubt it. I'm

hoping you'll find something to justify my hunch."

"I'll do my best," said Claire. But she admitted to herself that she hoped he wasn't.

". . .There is someone else I want you to look into."

"Another attractive man, I hope."

"Alas, no, a rather unpleasant middle-aged concierge."

"Variety is the spice of life," laughed Claire.

"The concierge, who prefers the title *gardienne*, of the building in which David lives dramatically altered her life style—new clothes, new furniture, a total makeover—just before David moved in. I'd like to know where the money for the changes came from."

"Probably an inheritance."

"That is what the residents suspect, and it may be the case. But if so I find it odd she never mentioned a funeral or showed any signs of mourning. And the timing—just before David moved in—is 'interesting.'"

"OK. I'll see what I can find out."

"You'll have to be sly; the woman is not inclined to chat."

Claire was not sure how effective she would be. Engaging young men was one thing, gaining confidences from elderly women quite another. From Clavel's description, she suspected Mme Langel was bitter about being a concierge and having to answer to residents she felt to be no better than herself. The models for the makeover had probably been those very residents.

She decided her best approach would be as one stylish woman to another. A few compliments on her taste in clothes and home décor might open the door to a wider conversation. Might.

Best, too, to show respect by arranging a meeting rather than simply appearing at her door. This done, she went home to dress for her new role. She pulled her hair into a tight chignon, put on a dark blue dress, hoping it was not too short, added a string of fake pearls and small silver earrings, and looked at herself in the mirror. She smiled, imagining what Olivier would have thought. Certainly nothing complimentary. But he was not her audience today.

It was a nice day, so Claire decided to walk the few short blocks to rue Cassett. It would give her time to get into her role. The route along rues Jacob and Bonaparte through the place Saint-Germain was lined with the sorts of shops at which she imagined Mme Langel had long wanted to shop and now did.

As she turned the corner onto rue Cassett, she was startled to see someone resembling Jacques entering the Pizza Chic restaurant on the corner. Was her imagination getting the better of her? The resemblance was certainly striking, but she couldn't risk trying to get a closer look in case it was he. She tried to put the thought out of her mind as she rang Mme Langel's bell.

The woman who opened the door fit the description Clavel had given her to a T. So too did her demeanor. Welcoming was not an adjective that came to mind.

"Good morning, Madame Langel. I'm sorry to have to bother you, but Commissaire Clavel has a few questions he thinks only you can answer."

"I already told him everything I know," replied Mme Langel without moving from in front of the door.

"Yes, you have been very helpful, and we appreciate it, but a number of new questions have come up that we think only you can help us with. It won't take long."

"Come in, then."

"What a lovely apartment," said Claire, looking around with what she hoped was evident admiration.

"Thank you."

"Oh, I adore your dining table and chairs. They're exactly what I'm looking for, although they're probably outside my budget. May I ask where you got them?" she gushed, walking around the table and running her hand over the surface.

"They were rather expensive but worth the price. Bon Marché only sells the best, you know. The table is by Saarinen and the chairs are Carl Hansen," replied Mme Langel with noticeable pride.

She had learned her lesson, reflected Claire, regretting that she herself knew so little about furniture design.

"Oh, I love Bon Marché. I love their shoe department, don't you?"

"Yes, I do, I buy all my clothes there, in fact."

"I did notice your dress—it's so chic."

Having elicited the first hint of a smile, Claire pulled out her notebook and asked a number of useless questions designed to justify her visit. This done, she closed the notebook, thanked Mme Langel for her time, and rose to leave. As she reached the door, she turned and looked back at the room.

"Your apartment is so beautiful. Did you study interior design?"

"No, I never had the chance, but my son studied at Beaux Arts, and he helped me redo the apartment."

Now we're getting somewhere, thought Claire.

"You are very lucky to have such a talented son. Do you think he might give me some advice? I'd pay him, of course."

"Oh, I don't think so. He isn't in the business, he's really a painter. These are his," she said, pointing to three mid-sized oils. One looked remarkably like a Matisse painting of olive trees that Claire had seen recently at the Orangerie. The other two reminded her of Braque.

"Lovely," said Claire, thinking that he had talent if not originality.

Claire headed back to her apartment to change before going into the office to brief Clavel. Passing the Pizza Chic, she peeked in the window and, not seeing the Jacques look-alike, went in, being careful to first put on the "disguise glasses" she always carried when doing investigative work. With large square lenses and blue and yellow frames, they were intended to attract attention and be the only thing people remembered about her.

She glanced around as if looking for someone. She signaled a waiter.

"I'm supposed to meet a friend here, but I don't see him. Is this your only room?"

"Yes."

"Strange. Do you know if Jacques Allard was here earlier? I am a bit late."

"Hey, François, you know a client by the name of Allard, Jacques?"

"Yes, why?" said a young man wearing designer jeans and a black T-shirt coming out of the kitchen.

"This lady's looking for him."

"I was supposed to meet him here, I'm a bit late. I wondered if he had come and gone or was late himself."

"He was here but left a good thirty minutes ago. If I were he, I would have waited," smiled François, looking approvingly at Claire.

She smiled back, shrugged, and left. She wondered how François would describe her to Jacques, because she was sure he would. If he focused on the glasses, it would be different from the descriptions she was sure the waiter at Pré aux Clercs and Olivier would give him. And what about Mme Langel—did she also know Jacques?

CHAPTER 14

I T WAS AFTER FIVE WHEN CLAIRE GOT BACK to the office. Mme Pinan had left for the day. In the absence of "the door-keeper," as she was known to the Clavel team, Claire knocked and entered without waiting for a response.

"Well?" asked Clavel, rising as she came in. Among the many things Claire admired about her boss were his old-fashioned manners. He even opened doors for women. Her feminist friends would have objected, but Claire was charmed.

"I didn't learn anything about the source of her wealth, but I did learn that she has a son, a painter, who studied at Beaux Arts and helped her redecorate her apartment. What struck me was how similar the style was to that of Olivier's apartment."

"Same interior designer?"

"Possibly More likely one of the same school. The style is so exactly what you would expect in Olivier's apartment, I suspect he did it himself."

"So you think the fact that Olivier and Madame Langel's son both studied at Beaux Arts would explain the similarities?"

"It could. And I wonder if they might even have collaborated on the two apartments. I'll try to find out. I'm meeting Olivier again on Saturday."

Clavel's smile indicated his approval. "Did you—"

"Hold on. Even more interesting is that I spotted Allard, Olivier's friend, in the pizza restaurant next door."

"Pizza Chic?" asked Clavel, recalling the outrageous prices.

"Yes. I thought I saw him go in just as I was going to see Langel. After my Q and A with her, I went back and asked the waiter if Allard had been there and was told he had left thirty minutes before."

"The man seems to appear with remarkable frequency. We obviously need to find out more about him."

"What did Luc learn?"

"Not much. Only that he came to Paris from Lyon, studied at Beaux Arts, and had an unsuccessful internship at a gallery. I was going to ask you to follow up, but I think I'll do so myself. You've had contacts with too many people in his orbit already."

"Hold on. Did you say he came from Lyon?"

"Yes, why?"

"Didn't you also tell me that Langel was from Lyon?"

"Right. But lots of people in Paris come from Lyon."

"And have sons who went to Beaux Arts?"

"As I said, we need to find out more about him," admitted Clavel. "I think you should chat up Langel some more. I'm convinced she knows a great deal more about this case than she is letting on."

CHAPTER 15

THE DANINE GALLERY WAS ONE of the smaller ones along rue de Seine. Also, judging from the window display featuring prints and multiples rather than oils, one of the less prestigious. Clavel thought this might explain why the owner had been willing to take on Allard, an unpromising Beaux Arts graduate.

"May I help you?" asked the young woman sitting behind a desk covered with prints.

"Good morning. May I speak to Madame Danine?" asked Clavel, removing his hat and wondering if the young woman was proving to be a more satisfactory assistant than Allard.

"You are doing so," she said with a smile, indicating he was not the first person to make the mistake. "How may I help you? Are you looking for something special?"

"No, I'm afraid I have come to ask you a few questions," replied Clavel, pulling out his badge.

"Is this about Monsieur Allard?"

"Yes, it is. I know you already spoke with my colleague

but I'd like to ask you a few more questions."

"Certainly, certainly. Please sit down," said Madame Danine, pulling a chair out from a back room.

Good, reflected Clavel, she seems excited about being involved in a police investigation, or maybe just bored. Either way she'll try to be helpful.

"You told my colleague that Monsieur Allard worked here for only a short time, and that you found him unsatisfactory. In what way was he unsatisfactory?"

"In *every* way. He often arrived late and left early, and when he was here spent his time on his cell phone. He once even asked a client to wait while he finished a conversation. A personal conversation!"

"How rude."

"Rude and unprofessional. He was a most unpleasant person, but I had no idea he was a criminal. Imagine, I was often alone with him here."

"He may not be. Whether or not he has committed a crime is what we are trying to find out."

"Innocent until proven guilty?"

"Absolutely. At the moment we are just trying to find out more about him. Do you know where he worked after leaving you?"

"No. He knew better than to ask me for a reference. Maybe he decided to become a painter. He told me in his uniquely arrogant way that he 'had talent,'" she said dismissively.

"You say he was often on his cell phone. Did you ever

happen to overhear what he was talking about or to whom?"

"Most of the time he was just listening to the person on the other end, interjecting words here and there."

"Words?" said Clavel encouragingly.

"Yes, I heard him say the word 'Fauves' several times, so he must have been talking to someone about art. Fauves are—"

"Early twentieth-century artists," interrupted Clavel with a smile.

"Ah, a well-educated policeman."

"Just learning on the job. Did you ever catch a name of a person he was talking to?"

"The only one I remember is George, because that was my father's name."

"Do you recall anything else?"

"I'm not sure, but I think I heard him say Valon once."

"Valon?"

"I'm not absolutely sure but that's what it sounded like. It struck me because it's the name of a very high-end gallery on rue Matignon, and I can't imagine them having anything to do with someone like Allard."

"Does the gallery specialize in Fauves?"

"They specialize in modern European masters, which would include Fauves."

Interesting, thought Clavel. Why hadn't the doctor included it in the list of galleries he had suggested Clavel visit?

"Have you heard anything from or about him since you let him go?"

"No. And I'm just as glad."

"Well, thank you, you've been most helpful. If you re-member anything more about him, please contact me," said Clavel, handing her his card.

CHAPTER 16

NEW MORNING WAS OBVIOUSLY a more exclusive jazz club than Jeannette's and most others in the area. The doorman—or bouncer, depending on the circumstances—was not the grubby thug one saw posted in front of most clubs. This one was dressed in well-fitting black jeans and a sparkling white turtleneck. Rather than search her bag as they had done at Jeannette's, he merely asked for her name, checked it off a list, and informed her, "Monsieur is sitting by the piano."

He need not have told her, because Olivier stood up and waved as soon as she crossed the threshold. She wondered if the doorman didn't have a signaling device. More likely, Olivier was simply eager to see her. Or so she hoped.

As she threaded her way among the tables, she noticed that the crowd was in keeping with the doorman, or vice versa. Most were under thirty and stylishly but not flamboyantly dressed. Many of the women's handbags, expensive handbags, were hung on the backs of their chairs. Theft clearly was not a concern here.

"You look lovely," said Olivier, pulling out her chair. "What would you like to drink? I'm having a Black Russian."

"In keeping with your heritage?" asked Claire with a laugh.

"How did you know I was Russian?"

"You just have that exotic look," replied Claire, ruffling his hair.

"A Manhattan," she said, turning to the waiter.

"Are you from New York?" asked Olivier with a big grin.

"Do I look it?"

"Right out of *Sex and the City*."

Before Claire could think of a comeback, the waiter appeared with her drink.

"To us," said Olivier, raising his glass.

"To you," she replied, raising her glass and taking a sip. "But who are you? What do you do when you're not at a night club?" she asked, stroking his arm, hoping she sounded flirty rather than inquisitive.

"At the moment, I design handbags."

"At the moment?"

"I'm working on something that hopefully will allow me to quit. I want to be my own boss."

"I can sympathize. I keep hoping I'll win the lottery. Then I'd quit my job and live a life of leisure."

"Let's dance," said Olivier, rising and taking her hand.

Olivier was a superb dancer, and Claire decided to forget the case and enjoy the evening. She already had learned more than she had hoped, and probing further would only set off alarm bells.

As she snuggled next him in the cab on the way to his apartment, Claire wished Olivier had not told her about his "plan." Had he not, had he left any doubt in her mind that he had a role in the Barber case, she would have looked forward to the rest of night. Now, however, she had to overcome her own as well as his desire and ask to be taken home, and in a way that would not cut off future dates. It was Saturday, so having to go to work early the next day was out. The migraine line had become a cliché, but she couldn't think of anything better. His reaction was the predicted disappointment tinged with anger. When they reached her apartment, he leaned over and opened her cab door in silence. Her attempt at a last kiss was rebuffed.

"Damn," mumbled Claire as she let herself in. "Damn, damn, damn."

CHAPTER 17

TO JERSEY'S SURPRISE AND ANNOYANCE, the Buffalo News had refused to assign a reporter to the Barber story, so he decided to investigate it himself. If his suspicions were correct, any number of publications would be interested in the story. He'd free-lanced early in his career and found the prospect of doing so again energizing. He was glad for an excuse to "do"—and to prove that teaching and doing were not mutually exclusive.

He was also glad that he spoke decent French, thanks to his first wife. It was among the few things he thanked her for. He had met Sylvie when vacationing in Brittany. She had been a waitress at a restaurant in Quimper, and was what tabloids of the time would have referred to as a "blonde bombshell"— slim, buxom, and flirtatious. She was also an imaginative lover. She knew more ways of making love than all the other women he had known combined. She also knew how to spend money, although she hid this talent until after they were married. Within two years, she had drained Jersey's bank account. After several months of at times violent arguments, she asked for a divorce. Jersey had happily agreed and, thanks to his clever lawyer, she was denied alimony. At the time, he had been bitter, but now, happily single and financially secure, he felt the French lessons and the remarkable sex had been worth the hit to his then-meager savings.

The plane had reached cruising altitude and the seatbelt sign had been turned off. Jersey stood up and took his briefcase out of the overhead compartment. He pulled out copies of David's emails and the printouts he had made of the few thin stories in the French press that he had been able to find on the internet.

Rereading the latter confirmed his decision that his first stop had to be 36 quai des Orfèvres—the office of Commissaire Clavel of the Paris "BC," or *brigade criminelle*. That Clavel was in charge of the investigation was the only useful piece of information in the press. The police obviously were not inclined to confide in the media. That being the case, he decided to approach this Clavel, not as a reporter, but as a friend of David's who had potentially useful information and was eager to help in any way he could. All of which was true.

He looked at his watch. Seven and a half more hours. They were scheduled to land at 5:40 a.m. He had taken the same flight before and found that, at that hour, the lines at customs and immigration were relatively short. If he caught the first Roissy bus into town, he would be at his hotel before 9:00 and at Clavel's office by 10:00. His plan was to catch the police by surprise, not give them an opportunity to direct him to some obscure staffer whose job was to sort through the reams of mostly useless "leads" people submitted in such cases. If he could just get him to read the emails, he was sure the commissaire would talk to him. And once he did, Jersey was confident he'd be able to extract enough information about the investigation to conduct his own. He'd built his career on getting people to reveal information they had no intention of revealing. He smiled, remembering the time he had gotten a city councilman to admit to having taken a bribe. The guy was so enamored of his connections in the business community that he bragged about one of them having given him season tickets to the Buffalo Bills games. Connecting that to the award of a city contract had been easy.

Confident that no further preparation was necessary, he signaled the hostess to tell her he did not want a meal—not that what they called dinner merited the name—and to please not disturb him. He put on his eye mask, leaned the seat back, and was immediately asleep.

CHAPTER 18

CLAVEL WAS JUST GATHERING UP HIS NOTES for his Monday morning staff meeting when Mme Pinan knocked and stuck her head in.

"Commissaire, there's an American gentleman here who says he is a friend of Monsieur Barber. I told him you were busy, but he says he has come all the way from New York and has information you will find useful. I think you should talk to him."

Clavel glanced at his watch; he had ten minutes before the meeting. The normal procedure would have been to tell Mme Pinan to have the man make an appointment with one of his assistants. But Clavel rarely followed normal procedures and even more rarely went against Mme Pinan's advice. He also felt at a dead end and welcomed any information he could get.

"Have him come in. And buzz me in ten minutes."

Jersey straightened his tie and pushed the half-open door.

"Commissaire, thank you for seeing me. I understand you are busy, but I think you'll be interested in what I have to say," said Jersey, stretching out his hand.

"Please sit down," said Clavel, ignoring the outstretched hand and pointing to one of the two chairs in front of his cluttered desk. He took the other, looked at Jersey, and waited.

Jersey was familiar with the tactic. Silence made people uneasy; it encouraged them to talk, often saying things they had not intended to say. But two could play the game, and the police wanted information as much as he did. Moreover, he had the advantage of having the entire day free. Clavel did not. So he crossed his legs and gazed around the room.

"You said you have information about Monsieur Barber?" said Clavel, breaking the silence.

"Yes. David, Monsieur Barber, was a student of mine at journalism school—one of my best students, in fact. I read in the paper that he was assaulted, and I'm concerned."

"We are all concerned," replied Clavel, rising to indicate the meeting was over. He resented having been misled. The man was a journalist and was clearly seeking to obtain—not provide—information.

Jersey ignored the hint and remained seated. He knew, however, he had blundered. A change in tactic was called for. "I think I have information that might help solve the case."

"Go on," said Clavel, resuming his seat.

"As I said, David was a fine journalist. I was disappointed when he quit his journalism job and moved to Paris. But he assured me he was going to keep writing. We kept in touch sporadically via email after he came to Paris. Two weeks ago—that is, just before he was attacked—I received this email."

"I'm afraid I don't read English."

"Ah. Well he says he thinks he has stumbled on a big story about the art underworld, one that will jump-start his career. Given that he was attacked shortly after sending the email, perhaps his attackers wanted to silence him."

"A fair assumption," acknowledged Clavel. "What more does he say about his discovery?"

"He says he doesn't want to reveal too much over the internet but does say that it all started when he saw a photograph at an exhibit at Sotheby's by Norman Parkinson called *After van Dongen (photographed 1959, sale price $6,000-$9,000).* Photography is my hobby, so I guess he thought I'd be interested in that aspect. Here is a picture of that photograph."

"Van Dongen?"

"Yes, he is one of the Fauves, they're—"

"Yes, I know what they are," laughed Clavel.

Noting Jersey's puzzled look, Clavel explained that the term Fauve had come up repeatedly during the course of the investigation.

"In what context?" asked Jersey.

"Sorry," winked Clavel. "I can't share that with you, or any journalist."

"I'm not here as a journalist. In fact, I'm no longer a journalist, I'm a professor. And one who taught and became friends with David. And I'd like to help."

"And we welcome your help. May I have the email? I'd like to have it translated, officially translated."

"Of course. But I assure you my translation was accurate."

"I don't doubt it, but I'd like a copy for the file, a copy my staff can understand."

As if on cue, there was a knock on the door and Mme Pinan came in.

"Thank you, Madame. Tell the staff I'm on my way. And please have this document translated."

Jersey had risen in turn but made no move to leave, hoping Clavel would ask him to wait, or suggest a follow-up meeting. He'd be in a better position to ask questions if the police had requested the meeting than if he had.

"I regret but I have to attend a meeting with some of my staff," said Clavel, turning to Jersey and picking up his pile of notes. "Perhaps you can come back this afternoon, say 2:00 p.m., and meet with me and a member of my staff who is working on this case?"

"Of course," replied Jersey, accompanying Clavel out the door.

"Good-bye, Madame," said Jersey, bowing his head. I'll bring her flowers this afternoon—it's always a good idea to have the gatekeeper on your side, he thought, unwittingly adopting the staff's sobriquet for Mme Pinan.

CHAPTER 19

C LAIRE HAD SLEPT MOST OF SUNDAY, recovering from her evening with Olivier. She was exhausted, not so much from staying up all night or drinking too much, but from playing the role of a flirtatious but prudish secretary. It was a role for which she was ill-suited, and which she had played poorly. She had badly misjudged Olivier's tolerance for resistance and, after last night, she wasn't sure how she'd manage to see him again. But see him again she must. She now had no doubt he was involved in the crime, but his role remained a mystery. And she needed evidence, hard evidence that would stand up in court.

By the time she reached the office Monday morning, she had resolved to put Olivier out of her mind and to spend the day, after the staff meeting, looking into the auction of the Maren collection. David had wanted to talk with Mme Corez about the auction. Why? Was preventing him from doing so the motive for the crime? The timing suggested it.

Claire was familiar with the Drouot auction house. She had

spent many hours there browsing at the pre-sale exhibits during her time with Corbier's, when her focus had been the art market. On any day, you could count on finding at least one, and often several, exhibits. Unlike Christie's or Sotheby's, Drouot was basically a cooperative of auctioneers in which members rented rooms as needed for their auctions. They ranged from the equivalent of yard sales to events offering million-dollar art and jewelry.

With the help of Drouot's website, she was able to determine that there were eight auctions on the date the Maren collection was put on the block. The site provided the name of each auction house along with its phone number, email address, and pictures of the auctioned items. Of the eight, only two involved paintings, one "Asian Art" and one "Modern and Contemporary." A quick glance at the latter confirmed that it was the Maren collection auction. She recognized most of the items from the photos David had taken in the apartment.

Before she could decide what to do next, Clavel came into her office and plopped down onto the delicate Queen Anne loveseat Claire had moved into her office the year before. The sofa had been her mother's and had sentimental value but clashed with the other furniture in her apartment—all Danish modern.

"I had an interesting meeting this morning with an American who says he was a professor of Barber's. He claims to have information that would help in the investigation. He's coming back at two. I'd like you to join the meeting."

"With pleasure," answered Claire. "Why didn't you mention this at staff?"

"Because I don't know if it's not just a waste of time. If we learn anything, I'll certainly share it."

It was already 1:30, so lunch would have to be a take-away sandwich. That was no hardship. The bistro Le Sarah Bernhardt, just across the Seine on place du Châtelet, had the best ham-and-butter sandwich in Paris. Unlike so many places, they used a "baguette traditionelle," which made all the difference. They also were willing to sell for take-away, at least when a member of the *police judiciare* was concerned.

"Madame Simon, welcome—a table for one?" asked Gérard.

"No, thanks. Just a ham-and-butter to go."

"Busy time, I guess," he said, returning from the kitchen with the sandwich.

"Yes. I'm working on the Barber case," replied Claire, knowing he'd have heard of the case and knowing too that, in exchange for the special privileges accorded the police, the waiters expected information. She'd never give them confidential information, but there was no harm in speaking about what was, or would soon be, public.

"Any ideas who or why?"

"Unfortunately, we don't," Claire replied truthfully, although of course she had some ideas of her own. Ideas she wouldn't share even with Clavel until she had more evidence.

She ate her sandwich as she walked back to the office. She couldn't understand how anyone could eat a sandwich sitting at a table. Apples, ice cream cones, and sandwiches were foods to be eaten while walking. If you didn't need utensils, you didn't need to sit down, and you certainly didn't need a table, she often told friends, none of whom agreed with her.

Clavel certainly didn't. She found him in his office sitting at his desk, eating a sandwich.

"Tell me about this American," said Claire, taking one of the chairs in front of the desk.

"All I know is that he was a journalism professor of Barber's and has been in correspondence with him since he arrived in Paris, including just a few days before the assault. He gave me this email," replied Clavel, handing Claire a copy of the translated email and the photo of the *After van Dongen* photograph. "The meeting this afternoon is to see what additional information he might have. And I suspect, for him, it's a chance to find out what we know."

"Hm. So he's a journalist."

"He says 'was.' He is now a professor of journalism."

"But you think, once a journalist, always a journalist?"

"I do. But I welcome any help he can provide. We just have to be careful how much we reveal."

"This email alone is extremely helpful."

Before she could elaborate, there was a knock on the door and Mme Pinan announced Jersey's arrival.

Claire and Clavel looked at each other inquisitively. Each was wondering what had come over Mme Pinan. Her tight-lipped grimace had been replaced by a large toothy smile.

"Monsieur Jersey, this is Officer Simon—she's working on

the Barber case with me. Please have a seat," said Clavel, pointing to the set of armchairs arranged around a low glass coffee table he kept in the corner of his office for small meetings.

"I have shown her the email you left with me, and we agree that it supports our theory that David had uncovered questionable activity involving art, and that a possible motive for the assault was to silence him and destroy any evidence he may have had."

"That was my suspicion, and I'm glad to hear you have additional evidence to support it."

"Unfortunately, we can't share what we have with you at this time," said Clavel, answering Jersey's unspoken request.

"I understand," replied Jersey, disappointed but not surprised.

"That said, we would welcome any additional information you might have," said Claire with her most engaging smile.

"A one-way street?" said Jersey with a wink which he immediately regretted. This was not the time to joke or flirt. Maybe later, but not now.

"I'm afraid so. You said you had exchanged a series of emails with David. I hope we all can agree to use his first name. Would you be willing to share those with us?" asked Clavel.

"Of course. There are only five. They're in English—should I read them to you?" asked Jersey, pulling a manila envelope out of his briefcase.

"Perhaps you could summarize them, and then, if you agree, I'll have them translated."

"The first one is dated just after he arrived in Paris and says he's looking for an apartment and has reconnected with a high school girlfriend. He doesn't mention a name," said Jersey.

"We know her name," said Claire with an emphasis on the "we."

"Hm. Well, the next one is a month later, and he says he has found an apartment, but that he can't move in until the current owner dies. I assume you know that already."

"Yes."

"The third one talks about the owner of the apartment, a nice elderly man, and the fact that he had an extensive art collection."

"Is that all he says about the art?" asked Claire.

"In this email, yes. I was a bit surprised, because David always had an interest in art, and I would have expected him to say more. However, in the next email, which came about five months later, he says he has become friends with the owner, whom he refers to as Pierre, and that, learning that Pierre had no interest in the art on his walls, offered to buy one of the paintings. He says Pierre told him he was not free to do so because the art had belonged to his wife, and that, under her will, the entire collection was to go to her children on his death."

"Did he describe the painting he wanted to buy?" asked Clavel.

"No, unfortunately. Do you have an inventory of the paintings?"

Claire glanced at Clavel who simply shrugged, which she took to mean that he was leaving the decision to her.

"We have some photos David took of the apartment while Pierre was still alive. They are in our safe." The latter was not true; the photos were in fact in Clavel's desk, but she didn't want to show them to Jersey, not yet anyway. "We don't know if they capture every picture, but we're assuming they include the picture of particular interest to David. I'm telling you this because it will help you help us. We trust that you will not make this information public. In fact we ask that you not make anything we tell you public," explained Claire, in as severe a tone as she could manage. She was beginning to think she should have taken acting classes. Her natural inclination was to be charming, if not flirtatious, when dealing with attractive men. And this case had plenty of those, Jersey being the latest addition. She was taken by his tall, muscular build and easy-going, friendly manner. And his earlier wink had not escaped her. He wasn't magazine cover-handsome like Olivier but had a certain *je ne sais quoi*. And then there was the dark and mysterious Allard. An embarrassment of riches, and all out of her reach, she laughed to herself. Of course, the case would end and then. . . . She was brought back to reality on hearing her name.

"Thank you, Madame Simon, I appreciate your trust and assure you my only objective now is to help you solve the case," replied Jersey, hoping they did not notice the "now." In truth, he had no intention of violating their trust during the course of the investigation. If he wrote anything, it would be after the case had been solved.

"And the last email was the one you showed me this morning in which he mentions a photograph *After van Dongen*. Did you have any contact with David after that, a phone call per-haps?" asked Clavel, hoping to bring the conversation back to the topic of Jersey's interactions with David.

"No. I had hoped that his saying he didn't want to reveal more about his suspicions over the internet meant he would write me a letter with more details, but I haven't received one. And if he *had* written, even as late as the day he was attacked, I would have received it by now."

"How long do you plan on remaining in Paris?" asked Claire.

"As long as I can be of help. I'm entirely at your disposal."

"We appreciate that," said Clavel, rising to indicate that the meeting was over.

As she opened the door to show Jersey out, Claire stopped abruptly. Turning to Jersey, she raised her eyebrows and pointed at the large bouquet of flowers on Mme Pinan's desk. Jersey merely nodded.

"You've set a bad precedent," whispered Claire with a smile.

Walking back to his hotel, Jersey began to whistle. Things were going much better than he had expected, and for that he gave himself full credit. The flowers had been a brilliant coup—winning over Claire as well as Mme Pinan. From what he had seen, he figured that, as long as he had the confidence and support of Claire, he didn't have to worry about Clavel. It wasn't a case—as he had thought at first —of her having him wrapped around her little finger. Clavel was clearly the boss, but a boss who respected her opinion.

CHAPTER 20

WELL?" ASKED CLAVEL AS CLAIRE RETURNED to his office.

"I think I want to look more carefully at the pictures of the auctioned items I found on the internet and the photos David took of the apartment," said Claire, not wanting to comment on Jersey. She knew her professional opinion was tainted by her personal one.

"Because?"

"Because I bet at least one of them resembles a van Dongen. Bingo," said Claire holding up one of the photos Clavel had handed her.

"It doesn't look like the photograph Jersey showed us," commented Clavel, examining the photo, which was of a painting of a blossoming tree.

"No, it's not a picture of a woman in a red hat, but it's clearly a van Dongen," replied Claire, hoping not to sound too dismissive.

"If you say so." Clavel trusted Claire's expertise; it was one of the reasons he had hired her, but he couldn't for the life of him see any resemblance between the painting of a flowering tree and the photograph of a woman in a red hat.

Sensing his skepticism, Claire went to her office and brought back one of the many art books that filled her bookshelves. She stored them there largely because she didn't have room in her apartment ,but this was not the first time they had proven useful.

"Look, here is one van Dongen—*Corn Poppy*—that looks very much like the *After van Dongen* photograph Jersey showed us, and here is another van Dongen, *Spring*, that resembles the painting David photographed—same tree, different season."

Clavel nodded and smiled.

"This is very interesting. Let me read you what it says. '*Spring* was painted in 1908 and was originally owned by Sergei Shchukin, a Russian business man who had become an art collector. After the 1917 Revolution, the government appropriated Shchukin's collection and turned his mansion into the State Museum of New Western Art, which was closed in 1948 and its collection divided between the Hermitage and the Pushkin Museum of Fine Arts. Shchukin escaped to Paris in 1918.'"

"Sounds like a story I've heard before. We need to talk to Madame Corez. She may know more about the history of the Maren family's collection than she told me," said Clavel, reaching for the phone.

"First, look at this," said Claire, pointing to a painting of a tree on the printout she had made of the auction's online catalogue.

"Of course, the painting along with all the others in the collection was sold at the auction."

"Yes, but don't you see? The auctioned painting doesn't have the small scratch in the top corner that you can see on David's photo of the picture hanging in the apartment."

"Maybe the auctioneer, or Olivier, had it repaired in order to fetch a higher price."

"Maybe," Claire said. "Maybe not," she thought.

Back in her office, Claire compared each of David's photos with the images on the auction's website. The only instance where they were noticeably different was in the case of the van Dongen-like tree. If, as Clavel speculated, it had been repaired for the auction, then why weren't any of the other paintings repaired? Several showed signs of wear and tear. One had actually pulled away from the frame, and the paint had chipped off in several places on another.

Chapter 21

THERE BEING NO DESK IN HIS ROOM, Jersey sat down in front of the small dressing table intending to write a report, a report to himself, about the investigation. He picked up his pen, put it down, and went to the phone.

"Bonjour, this is Monsieur Jersey. May I speak to Madame. . .Officer Simon, please."

"Just a minute."

The delay gave him time to wonder if the call was a good idea. Was he moving too fast, being too aggressive? Having given his name, he couldn't very well hang up. Maybe he should just ask some useless question. Before he could think of one, Claire answered.

"Hello, have you made a discovery already?" she said with a laugh, a joyful not dismissive laugh.

"Yes, that I'd like to take you to dinner." Had he really said that? Jersey wondered.

Apparently so, because Claire accepted, and they agreed to meet at La Frégate. It was his choice. It had a spectacular view of the Seine and the Louvre, and offered better than average food at below average prices. And, most importantly, had large tables spaced well apart so they'd be able to talk without shouting and without being overheard.

Jersey arrived early to be sure they had reserved a table away from the door and in front of the windows as he had requested. He declined the waiter's suggestion that he order a cocktail, saying he'd order wine when his guest arrived. Staring out the window at the boats passing along the Seine, he remembered his first visit to France—the visit when he had met his wife and been introduced to a sex-centered world, a world in which nothing else seemed to matter. It hadn't ended well, but he had no regrets. Quite the opposite. He'd gladly live it over again if he could. With that thought, he abandoned his initial plans to use the dinner to obtain information about the case. This would be a purely social evening. If it went well, there would be plenty of time to discuss the case in the coming days.

Claire wasn't sure whether Jersey intended it to be a business or a social evening. She hoped it would be both. She couldn't think of a way she would prefer to spend the evening than dining with an attractive man in a romantic setting. As far as the case went, she hoped he would be able to help her play the starring role. If, as he claimed, his only interest was in helping find the culprits, he wouldn't mind if she got the credit. And even if his goal was, as Clavel suspected, to get a good story for a U.S. newspaper, he shouldn't mind her getting the credit for solving the case. She would even be willing to trade bits of information in exchange for his help.

As she took her seat opposite Jersey and he looked up and smiled, Claire knew that, socially, the evening was going to be a success. So did Jersey.

Over dinner of grilled bass accompanied by a chardonnay, they traded basic details about themselves. They were both single. They both enjoyed the theater and film. Neither was particularly fond of spectator sports. He enjoyed skiing. She would like to learn. She had a background in art. He wished he knew more. Neither mentioned the Barber case.

Their chitchat was interrupted by the waiter producing the bill and announcing that the restaurant was closing. Jersey was pleased that Claire made no attempt to pay her share of the bill. To have done so would have been a signal he did not want to receive.

As they left the restaurant, he took her hand. She squeezed it and led him down the rue du Bac, turning on rue de Lille and onto rue Allent. She no longer regretted giving up Olivier.

"Charming street for a charming woman," said Jersey, pulling her close and putting his arm around her shoulder.

"A nightcap?" she asked as she punched in the code to her building.

Jersey didn't bother to reply but merely followed her in and up the three flights to her apartment.

"Make yourself comfortable," she said, pointing to the sofa as she took off her coat.

He reached for the coat, threw it on the sofa, and drew her towards him.

JERSEY WOKE UP TO THE NOISE OF THE SHOWER. Stepping into the shower, he pressed his naked body against hers. This was the first time he had made love under a shower since his first trip to Paris. It was better than he had remembered.

"I've got to dress and go to work," said Claire, giggling and pulling away as he tried to carry her back to the bed.

"Lunch?" asked Jersey.

"Can't. I have lunch with Clavel every Tuesday."

"Lucky guy."

"You're not jealous, are you?" asked Claire, surprised by Jersey's tone and somber expression.

"Not if you tell me I have no cause."

"None at all," she replied, kissing him with the same passion she had shown the night before. "Meet me at five, here. The code is B3542, and here is a spare key."

CHAPTER 22

W E HAVE AN APPOINTMENT with Madame Corez at 2:00," announced Clavel as he and Claire left for lunch. "I want to find out more about the Maren collection."

"In that case let's go to Au Pied de Fouet on the rue Saint Benôit. It's on the way, and I'm in the mood for chicken livers," said Claire.

"I'm not—not in the mood for chicken livers," said Clavel with a grimace that made Claire laugh.

"Their *confit de canard* is superb," she said, knowing it to be one of his favorites.

"What's the plan?" asked Claire after they had placed their orders.

"I think you should ask her what she knows about the collector you read me about."

"Shchukin. And?"

"And hopefully she'll take it from there and compare the Shchukin collection to hers and the Marens'. If my hunch is correct, the Maren collection contained works similar to those in Shchukin's."

"And if the Maren works were not placed in a museum by the Soviets, they ended up in private collections or were not confiscated," said Claire, continuing Clavel's thought.

"Exactly."

"I hope your hunch is correct. As it usually is," said Claire, signaling the waiter to ask for a coffee and the check.

CHAPTER 23

CLAVEL HAD FORGOTTEN THE CODE to the street door, so they buzzed Mme Langel. She was obviously surprised, and not pleased, to see them. Her expression seemed to say "now what?"

Her relief was obvious when Clavel told her they were there to see Mme Corez.

Mme Corez was standing in her open doorway when they reached her apartment.

"Ah, I congratulate you, Commissaire, a female assistant. And so attractive."

"Officer Simon, glad to meet you," said Claire trying, unsuccessfully, not to show her annoyance. How long would it be before female police investigators were not considered oddities, and of what relevance were her looks? She told herself that Mme Corez was of a different generation and of course meant well. She was still annoyed.

Mme Corez addressed Clavel. "How may I help you today?"

"We have a few questions about the art collection of Madame Maren's father," replied Claire before Clavel could respond.

Clavel merely nodded. He wasn't about to get in the middle of this fight.

"And what, Officer Simon, do you want to know?" asked Mme Corez with uncharacteristic severity.

The tone caught Claire by surprise. Clavel had described Mme Corez as a witty, engaging woman. She looked at Clavel, who shrugged as if to say, "You started it."

"I understand from what Commissaire Clavel told me that Madame Maren's father was an art collector in Russia whose collection was largely confiscated before he fled at the time of the 1917 revolution."

"That is correct."

"Officer Simon, who is something of an art expert, was telling me about another Russian collector, a Monsieur Shchukin. It seems his collection ended up in the Hermitage after the 1917 Revolution. Do you know if any of the Maren collection also found its way to a museum?" inquired Clavel, hoping to change the atmosphere.

Mme Corez smiled. She understood from Clavel's compliment that he was trying to excuse Claire's rudeness, and she was happy to accept.

"Jewish art collectors were a close-knit group in Russia at the time of the revolution, and both my and Madame Maren's father had known Shchukin. The Shchukin collection was in a class by itself, its value far surpassing those of other collectors.

I remember visiting his mansion in Moscow when I was a child. The house was like a museum. Shchukin himself conducted public tours," explained Mme Corez with the enthusiasm she must have felt as a child. In 1918, Lenin confiscated the entire collection and moved it to museums. At least the scoundrel recognized the value. Later, Stalin moved some work to the Pushkin Museum in Moscow and the rest to the Hermitage in St. Petersburg. But you probably know all this."

"I had not known he had turned his home into a virtual museum," replied Claire. "Did other collectors do the same?"

"Not that I know of, and certainly not my or Irene's, Madame Maren's family. I was only a child, but I recall the awe with which the Shchukin collection was spoken. We had some valuable works, but the collection as a whole was not museum quality. From what I understood, neither was that of Irene's family."

"Do you know if any of the works in your or the Marens' collection ended up in a museum?"

"Not that I'm aware. I think everything ended up in private Bolshevik hands. That was the case of most confiscated works. The Shchukin collection was really in a different category from those of other collectors. And the Bolsheviks recognized that."

"I understand the Shchukin collection contained a number of Fauves, which must have run against established taste at the time."

"Oh, my, yes," said Mme Corez, laughing and shaking her head. "We also had some works of the Fauve school, but no big names. Our friends were shocked that we hung such things in our house."

"Were they confiscated?"

"No. They left us the few we had. As you said, they were not in favor. They took the Shchukins simply because they were Shchukin's. They took his entire collection, whereas in most cases they sorted out the 'good' from the 'worthless.'"

"Did the Marens also have Fauves?" asked Claire, holding her breath and crossing her fingers.

"As I've said, I'm not familiar with their entire collection, but Irene did say she wished her family had collected more Fauves. Which I guess would imply they had some."

"And that those they had were not confiscated?"

"I had never thought about it, and I never noticed any obvious Fauves on Irene's walls, but I guess that must be the case, or why would she care how many they had?" replied Mme Corez, raising her eyebrows as if to say, "See, I'm smart enough to follow your logic."

Claire simply nodded .

"Well, we don't need to take any more of your time," said Clavel, rising.

"It's been a pleasure. I do hope you catch the thugs."

"Thanks to your help, we will," said Claire.

Mme Corez laughed and said, "Even unjustified compliments are welcome."

It was raining when Claire and Clavel left the building. Because he wanted Claire's opinion before she had time to edit it, Clavel suggested that, rather than go back to the office, they have a coffee at the boulangerie around the corner. He might even indulge in another one of their *babas au rhum*. Over the years they had worked together, he had learned that Claire's initial reaction to an event or meeting was often very perceptive. When she had time to think things over, the key points got lost in complex analysis.

"We just made a giant leap forward," said Claire as soon as they had ordered. "My guess is that the painting of a tree that was hanging in the apartment, and that David photographed, was a genuine van Dongen, considered 'worthless' and not worth confiscating."

"Well, that certainly seems to be a giant leap from what Madame Corez told us," remarked Clavel.

"No. Not if you combine what she told us with what we already know."

"OK. Let's assume you are correct—where does that lead us in the investigation?"

"I need to think more about it. You do the same ,and let's talk tomorrow."

"Have evening plans?" said Clavel with a wink.

"Yes. I guess I can't fool you. But I do need to think it through."

"See you at 9:00 tomorrow, and don't over-analyze," said Clavel picking up the check and shooing her out the door.

CHAPTER 24

S HE HAD JUST FINISHED BLOW-DRYING her hair when Jersey walked in. Claire was surprised that he was empty-handed. She thought flowers would have been appropriate. Hiding her disappointment, she put her hands on his shoulders and kissed him on the cheek. He put his arm around her and turned to open the front door. There on the small landing was a large glass vase full of yellow and white roses.

Before she could respond, he had her in his arms and had kicked the door shut.

"They'll wait," he said. And wait they did.

As Claire was preparing dinner, Jersey rescued the flowers and distributed them among several of Claire's vases.

"I'm not much of a cook," said Claire, placing a platter of grilled salmon, surrounded by green beans and a baguette, on the table.

"I'll be the judge of that," said Jersey, opening the bottle of wine he had put in the fridge earlier in the day when Claire was at work.

"To us," said Claire, raising her glass.

"To us," replied Jersey, clinking his glass against hers.

"Are you real?" he asked.

"Excuse me?"

"Are you real, or am I having the most marvelous dream?"

"It's a marvelous dream come true."

They both laughed, and he rubbed his bare foot up and down her leg under the table.

"What did my dream lady do today?"

Claire described the meeting with Mme Corez but did not tell him her hunch about the painting.

"Do you think David's seller—Pierre, I think was his name—owned a valuable Fauve?"

Claire hesitated before answering. She wasn't sure how much she should tell him. She was inclined to share everything. She trusted him and wanted his help. But she knew Clavel would not have wanted her to even describe the meeting, let alone reveal their theories.

She comprised with, "I don't know. It's possible but we have no evidence."

"Got it," said Jersey. He understood her dilemma and read her answer as affirming his hunch.

"Shall we go for a walk? I haven't been in the Tuileries this trip."

"Absolutely. It's magical in the evening. I'll show you my favorite spot."

They were about half way along the main alley leading from the Louvre to the Place de la Concorde when Claire turned left and pointed to what Jersey thought was a fallen tree. She laughed at his puzzled expression.

"It's a sculpture. You can walk on it, sit on it, lie on it. I sometimes come here and curl up on that branch and read. Its one of the more peaceful spots in Paris. Most people don't even bother to stop and look at it. They all seem to be rushing to the Musée d'Orsay just across there or the Orangerie up there."

"Fools like me," said Jersey, pulling her close. "I've been in these gardens many times and never noticed your tree."

"Let's sit for a moment," said Claire, climbing onto the log.

Closing her eyes, she put her head on Jersey's shoulder and began to hum an aria from the *Marriage of Figaro*. Jersey smiled, wondering if a message was intended. He responded by humming the aria in which Cherubino describes his emerging infatuation for the Countess. Claire squeezed his hand and got up.

"Let's go home."

JERSEY WOKE BEFORE CLAIRE. It was only 6:00 a.m., so he slipped carefully out of bed so as not to wake her. He had noticed a boulangerie just down the block and decided to surprise Claire with breakfast of fresh croissants. He must have been one of the first customers, because the baker had to go into the back to get the croissants. They were still warm.

Claire was sleeping when he got back to the apartment. He put the pastries on a plate, undressed, and crawled back into bed. She opened her eyes and reached out to ruffle his hair.

"No, I have to get up or I'll be late to work," she said, pushing him away with a giggle.

"Breakfast first," Jersey said getting up and coming back with the plate of croissants.

"Oh, Jersey!" exclaimed Claire, clapping her hands like a little girl. "Breakfast in bed, how splendid. You stay here, I'll make some coffee."

"Look," said Claire, coming back into the bedroom, "I even have a tray with little legs."

Jersey felt a pang of jealousy as he wondered if she often had breakfast in bed. It was not something one tended to do alone.

"I got it when I broke my leg and had to stay in bed," she said, as if she had read his mind.

They ate in silence, each enjoying the moment.

Jersey broke it as he took the last bite of his croissant.

"What should I do while you're at work?"

"Whatever you want," said Claire. She was ashamed at having thought she would use him to help her solve the case.

"What I really want is to be with you," he said, taking her hand. "And if I can't be with you, then I want to at least be doing something to help you. And don't forget, I have my own interest in the case."

Claire wondered briefly if he wasn't using her but put the idea out of her mind. It wasn't credible, not after the last two days.

"Well, it would be helpful if we knew more about David.

Clavel thinks the victim holds the key to solving any crime. Maybe you could write down everything you know about David, even things that seem totally irrelevant."

"I'll give you a report this evening. By the way, I'm taking you to one of my favorite bistros."

Claire laughed at how confident he was about their relationship.

After Claire left for work, Jersey went to his hotel and checked out. He knew he was being presumptuous and that he should have waited for her to suggest he move in. But he was sure she would be pleased that he wanted to move in. Just in case he was wrong, he left his bags, packed, by the front door. That way, if she showed any displeasure, he could easily say he had decided to find a better hotel.

That settled, he sat down at Claire's dining room table and began to jot down what he knew about David. In less than an hour, he had four pages of notes. Other than David's recent emails, which he had already discussed with the police, none of it seemed the least bit relevant. But he knew that the seemingly irrelevant could become key when combined with other information. He could only hope the police had such Other Information.

Closing his notebook, he decided to visit some art galleries. He enjoyed looking at paintings and, since the case seemed to involve an art scam, he might just stumble on something important. As he headed toward the avenue Matignon, he felt twenty years younger. No longer a middle-aged professor but a young investigative journalist. A young investigative journalist in love.

His first stop was the Tamenaga Gallery. Its window displayed works by an artist named Aizpiri. He wasn't familiar with the artist but was enchanted with the colorful paintings of clowns and flowers. The owner eagerly explained that Aizpiri had worked with Picasso, and that his paintings could be classified as somewhere between Expressionism and Fauvism.

"Do you have other works by Fauves?" asked Jersey, delighted that he might already have stumbled on something of relevance to *the* case.

"Not at the moment. But if you are particularly interested in Fauves, you might want to visit the Valon Gallery just down the block."

The window of the Galerie Valon contained three large oil paintings by Albert Marquet. Jersey recognized the name as one Claire had mentioned as being a member of the Fauve movement. Contemplating the works, and thinking of Claire, he decided on a plan of action that might uncover some useful information.

"Bonjour, may I help you?" asked the young man appearing from what Jersey supposed was an office at the back of the gallery.

"Yes. I understand the gallery specializes in twentieth-century artists, and that you might have works by members of the Fauve movement."

"Yes. As you see, we have several rare works by Marquet," said the young man pointing to those in the window.

"Yes. They are magnificent. Would you happen to have

works by van Dongen?" Jersey asked.

"Yes, a wonderful artist. We do have one of his paintings, an unusual landscape, but we are having it reframed. If Monsieur would give me his information, I could contact you when it is ready."

"How long will that be? I'm only in Paris for a few weeks."

"Just a minute, I'll find out," said the young man retreating to the office.

Almost immediately, another young man appeared, smiling in a way only those hoping to make a lucrative sale do.

After a brief discussion, Jersey agreed to come back in a week to see the newly framed van Dongen. He did not give them his name or contact information.

He left the gallery feeling victorious. He had a sense that this van Dongen was important to resolving the case. If only the police had shared more information with him, he would know exactly how important it was. Maybe now they, or at least Claire, would confide in him. In fact, he reflected, his discovery might be the start of a Claire–Jersey collaboration. He took a skip at the thought. Ever since he could remember, joy had prompted him to skip. He wasn't displeased at still being able to do so but regretted that he had been observed by an obviously astonished young man passing him on the sidewalk.

It was still early so he decided to visit the Musée Nissim de Camondo, a small, elegant museum of decorative arts housed in the 1911 Camondo mansion. He recalled it as a wonderful place into which to escape because, unlike the large museum of decorative arts next to the Louvre, it was maintained as if it were still a private home. It was possible to imagine oneself eating at the elegantly set dining room table or relaxing with a book in the library.

As he walked up the rue Messine, he noticed the young man who had observed his skip entering an art gallery. As he got closer, Jersey noticed it was the Troubetzkoy Gallery. He knew the name. It was famous as among the world's best for producing copies of famous paintings. It had been established by a Russian prince whose friends had expressed an interest in having copies made of their collections, which they could hang when they loaned out the originals. The copies were always identified as such. The gallery made clear it was not in the forgery business.

He would have liked to visit but noticed the sign on the door said "closed." The young man must work there, he thought, proceeding on his way to the museum.

CHAPTER 25

"BONJOUR," CLAIRE CALLED OUT, ENTERING the Moquand auction house offices.

"Just a minute," replied a male voice from behind a large Chinese screen.

Looking around, Claire noticed a large number of paintings leaning against the walls, presumably the contents of an upcoming auction. Many were still lifes and appeared to be in rather poor condition. One, she noticed with pleasure, had a small tear. Another a broken frame.

"Bonjour, Madame, sorry to have kept you waiting. How can I help you?" said a short, portly man in a three-piece suit emerging from behind the screen. His deep-set gray eyes seemed to take her in, to estimate her. She hoped he saw a wealthy potential client.

"I would like to discuss the possibility of your auctioning my family's art collection."

"Certainly, certainly. Please won't you sit down," he said, pointing to a pair of rather worn leather chairs. "Tell me something about the collection."

Claire described a collection similar to that of the Marens.

"From what you say, I think we would be interested in working with you. Of course, I can't give you an estimate without seeing the collection."

"I understand. My concern is that several of the works were damaged in a recent move. My brother thinks they should be repaired before we sell them. I'm not sure—what do you think?"

"I can't say for certain without seeing the works in question, but in general I do not advise clients to undertake repairs. Poorly done, they can decrease the value of a painting, and, even well done, you probably won't recoup the cost. To be honest, I have never suggested a client have a work repaired. Of course, some clients have works repaired before ever coming to me. In that case I can only silently regret their having done so."

"Thank you. I'll talk to my brother and be back in touch," she said, leaving the gallery.

"I look forward to that, Madame. . . ?"

Claire ignored the question.

So he hadn't repaired the painting. Then who had? Wondering how she could find out, Claire walked down the rue Milton and took a small detour to the rue des Martyrs to buy some pastries at Landemaine. She didn't get to this neighborhood often, but she disagreed with Clavel that it had suffered from gentrification. She didn't see a problem with a string of high-end food shops and fancy clothing boutiques.

How could Clavel, a self-proclaimed gourmet, object to Landemaine, one of the best pastry shops in Paris, or Au Bon Port, with its vast selection of fresh fish and seafood? She was tempted to buy some turbot but then remembered Jersey had said he planned to take her to dinner. Crossing the Boulevard Haussmann, she spotted a tourist sign pointing to the Opéra Comique. "Why not?" she said to herself.

Fortunately there was no line at the box office, and the two clerks seemed eager to answer her questions. Not like the last time she tried to buy tickets—then, the sales clerk had rudely told her she was holding up the line and should come back when she knew what she wanted. She'd left without buying a ticket and hadn't been back since, and that'd been over a year before. Not wanting to tempt fate by assuming Jersey intended to stay in Paris for the indefinite future, she asked what was playing the following Friday. On being told it was Boieldieu's *La Dame Blanche,* she laughed out loud. It was too perfect, an opera in which the central dramatic focus is an auction scene. OK, it was the auction of a chateau, not a painting, but still. She bought two orchestra seats. On her own, she would have opted for the balcony, but decided it was best not to reveal her frugal instincts this early in their relationship.

CHAPTER 26

JERSEY HAD RESERVED A TABLE AT ALLARD, an elegant Michelin-starred restaurant on the rue Saint-André des Arts. "Allard?" asked Claire with surprise when he told her.

"Is that a poor choice? We can go elsewhere," he said, trying not to sound disappointed. He had assumed she would be pleased.

"Oh, no, it's a wonderful choice. It's just interesting because one of the characters in the Barber case is named Allard."

"Wow. I wonder if I have a sixth sense or something," laughed Jersey. "You'll have to tell me about him. But not now. We need to be off. The reservation is for 8:00, and it's already 7:45."

The maitre d' ushered them to their table, and an elderly waiter immediately presented them with a plate of complimentary hors d'oeuvres.

"If we eat all these, we won't need dinner," said Claire, reaching for a cheese-filled pastry.

"What would they do if we asked for a doggie bag?" joked Jersey.

"Throw us out!" she laughed, leaning over and giving Jersey a kiss.

Their banter was interrupted by the reappearance of the waiter bearing menus and a wine list. After listing the specials of the day and asking if they wanted an aperitif, which they declined, he left them to study the extensive menu.

"What tempts Madame?" asked Jersey.

"Everything, but especially the poached turbot. I want to test if theirs is better than mine. And it's my favorite fish."

"I'm tempted by the seared scallops. Would you share an order of snails with me to start?"

"With pleasure. Garlic for one, garlic for all," answered Claire with the wry smile Jersey had come to adore.

"Fish and scallops means white wine. I'm not a wine connoisseur—you select," said Jersey, handing Claire the wine list.

"I can't wait to see the waiter's expression when I order the wine," laughed Claire. "He seems very old school."

If the waiter was surprised at the woman's ordering the wine, he didn't show it. But he did suggest that they might prefer a chenin blanc rather than the pinot grigio Claire had chosen. Jersey thanked him but said they would have the wine Madame had selected.

"As you like," said the waiter, bowing his head slightly but in a tone that indicated he thought they would regret their choice.

"I think you offended him," said Claire.

"I offended him? I'd say he offended you."

"Well, thanks for taking my side," said Claire, taking Jersey's hand in hers.

Before he could respond, the waiter reappeared with the wine. He ceremoniously poured a swallow in a glass and handed it to Jersey to taste. Jersey, staring at the waiter, handed the glass to Claire, who sipped it and nodded to the waiter. He filled both their glasses, put the bottle down with just enough force to indicate his opinion of Jersey but not so much as to open himself to accusations of being rude, and left without a word.

Claire was amused at the battle of wills between Jersey and the waiter but said nothing. Instead she asked Jersey about his day.

"I may have made a discovery," said Jersey and proceeded to describe his visit to Valon Gallery.

"You said the name of the gallery was Valon?" asked Claire

"Yes, do you know it?"

"No, but the name has come up," said Claire, wondering again how much she could reveal to him.

"Look. I can't help you if you don't share what you know with me," replied Jersey, clearly annoyed.

Before she could respond, the waiter reappeared with the snails.

"Delicious," said Claire, scooping a snail from its shell.

Jersey just watched her, waiting for a response.

"OK, you're right," said Claire, putting down her fork.

"But let's enjoy this lovely meal first. I promise to tell you everything I know once we get home."

Jersey smiled and scooped up a snail. "Yes, delicious."

During the rest of the meal they talked of food. Jersey regaled Claire with stories about the diners where he ate during a cross-country trip he had taken during his college years. She had a hard time envisioning the jukebox-equipped booths, paper place mats, and plastic-coated menus and wondered how people could drink coffee with a meal of fried chicken and fries. She was also skeptical when Jersey said that "buffalo wings" were worth a trip to the U.S.

It was close to midnight by the time they left the restaurant. Having enjoyed two bottles of wine, neither a chenin blanc, they walked contentedly arm in arm back to Claire's apartment.

As she turned the key in the lock, she turned and asked Jersey if he liked opera.

"Yes, why?" asked Jersey, thinking it an odd question.

"Because we're going on Friday."

"We are?"

"Yes. The Opéra Comique is doing *La Dame Blanche*. I bought tickets this afternoon," she said, pointing to the envelope on the hall table.

"What a wonderful idea. I've never been to the Opéra Comique," Jersey said, plopping down on the sofa and patting the seat next to him. "You promised."

"Yes, 'promises made, promises kept,'" interrupted Claire. Lying with her head on his lap, she spent the next hour telling him everything she knew about the Barber investigation, including her own opinions about the key players.

"Does Clavel agree with your views?"

"For the most part, but he thinks Lotan is involved and I'm not so sure."

"You both think this Allard played an important role?"

"Yes, although we don't know what role. And I think once we figure that out the rest will fall in place."

"Remarkable that I just stumbled on the Valon gallery," said Jersey half to himself.

"Maybe you have the magical sixth or seventh sense," said Claire, kissing his hand, which was lying on her breast.

"All my senses are exhausted. Let's go to bed. We can figure out a plan tomorrow."

CHAPTER 27

IN PREPARATION FOR HIS VISIT to Lotan's tobacco shop, Clavel had read a short book on tobacco that Mme Pinan had managed to obtain from the library. He thought he knew enough to pass as a "sophisticated pipe smoker" interested in exploring new blends. And he hoped the few leaves he had from the crime scene were of a rare yet identifiable variety.

The shop was conveniently located just blocks from rue Madame. The window displayed a rack of pipes of various shapes and sizes. Over the door was a metal sign in the shape of a pipe on which the legend *This Is a Pipe* was written. Clavel viewed this play on René Magritte's famous painting as a pretentious indication that the shop hoped to attract an "up-scale" clientele, people who would pride themselves on understanding the reference. Snobs like the doctor.

Chimes announced Clavel's entrance. A tall, extremely thin young man with a goatee immediately appeared through the doorway behind the counter. He was wearing a greenish suit and had a pale yellow scarf knotted at his neck. Pretentious, like his sign, thought Clavel.

Handing the tobacconist the few tobacco leaves he had taken from the lab, Clavel explained that he had discovered the brand on a recent trip to London and wanted to renew his supply. Playing to the young man's ego, he added that he had been told that, if anyone in Paris had this brand, it would be this shop.

Taking the leaves, the tobacconist first smelled them and then laid them on the counter and examined them with a magnifying glass.

"You have excellent taste. And you're in luck. I ordered four boxes last month for another client who in the end only bought two."

"So, I'm one of only two people in Paris who appreciate this brand?" asked Clavel.

"I think so. I have not sold to anyone else, and I very much doubt any other tobacconist has this brand. I think we are unique in the variety of rare, high-end varieties we carry."

"I'm certainly glad I discovered you."

"Would Monsieur like both boxes or only one?"

"One will suffice, thank you," replied Clavel, wondering again how the budget office would react to an expense report featuring even one box of fancy tobacco, along with a designer handbag.

CHAPTER 28

C LAIRE WOKE UP BEFORE JERSEY and slipped out of the apartment without waking him. She wanted to discuss Jersey's role in the case with Clavel. She was quite sure he would agree to let her work with him and was absolutely sure he would be hurt and angry if she didn't ask his permission.

When she arrived at police headquarters, she went directly to Clavel's office. He had just arrived, and his door was open.

"May I come in?" she asked.

"Yes, I was going to call you. I have some interesting news."

"As do I."

"You first, then."

"You told me that Madame Danine, the gallery owner, told you that she overheard Allard refer to the Valon art gallery?"

Clavel nodded.

"Well, it seems Valon has a van Dongen landscape that it is having reframed, and that will be back in the gallery next week."

"And you think it may be the painting David purchased at the auction?"

"No, I think it is the painting that was in the Maren collection, and that David thought he was buying."

"*Thought* he was buying?"

"Yes. Remember I pointed out to you that the painting David photographed in the apartment had a scratch, and that the one shown in the auction catalog didn't?"

"Yes, and as I said then, I suspect it was repaired for the auction."

"I don't think so. I spoke with the auctioneer, and he said he never recommends clients repair paintings for auction and never did so himself."

"But Olivier might have had it repaired without telling the auctioneer, or against his advice."

"True, but I doubt it. Several of the paintings were in poor condition, and none were repaired. Why would he repair just this one?"

"Good point."

"Now, what's your news?"

"That Dr. Lotan lied when he said he was never in the apartment after David moved in."

"How did you reach that conclusion?" asked Claire, raising her eyebrows with skepticism.

"Remember the tobacco leaves that were found in the apartment, under a table? Well, according to the tobacco shop that Lotan frequents, it's a rare variety not sold elsewhere in

Paris, and for which the shop has only one client, whose name he would not reveal."

"And you think that one client is Lotan?"

"I do."

"Let's assume you're right, that the Doctor was the source of the tobacco in the apartment. Do we know that the tobacco was not there before David moved in?"

"How likely is that, given how thoroughly apartments are cleaned after a sale?" asked Clavel rhetorically.

"OK, but even if he was in the apartment after David moved in, where does that get us? Just having been in the apartment doesn't link him to the crime."

"No, but the fact that he denied having been there suggests his visit was not for laudable purposes," said Clavel.

"True. What do you think his purpose was?"

"I'm not sure, but I wouldn't be surprised if it had something to do with the painting David purchased at the auction."

"Because. . . ?"

"Because he's an art collector with an expertise in twentieth-century artists. And was clearly not pleased when Madame Corez revealed that fact."

"How do you plan to proceed?"

"I don't know. Any suggestions?"

"No, but I think we could use some help on this case."

"I agree, but the rest of the team are working on other cases."

"I see," said Claire. She paused before adding, as if the thought had just occurred to her, "Maybe we could involve

Jersey."

"The American journalist?" said Clavel with obvious surprise.

"The American friend of David's."

"Who is a journalist."

"Was. And he is here to help solve the case, not write about it."

"So he says."

"Why can't you believe him?" replied Claire, unable to hide her annoyance.

Clavel got up and walked to the window. Looking down on the street with his back to Claire, he thought back over his several meetings with Jersey. He had to admit that the man seemed sincere. He also had to admit that they needed help. The case was too complex for just Claire and himself. He also trusted Claire's judgment about people, even attractive men.

"OK," he said, turning back to look at Claire. "Can you arrange a meeting for the three of us later today."

"Yes," said Claire, rising.

"And thanks," she added as she opened the door to leave.

CHAPTER 29

URING HER LUNCH BREAK, CLAIRE WENT BACK to her apartment. She found Jersey sitting on the sofa with a laptop propped on his lap, sipping a glass a wine. Claire sat down next to him, put her arm around his shoulder, bit his earlobe, and whispered, "We're colleagues."

Responding to his quizzical look, she added, "I spoke to Clavel. We're all to meet this afternoon to plan our next steps."

"Let's celebrate," he said, picking her up and carrying her into the bedroom.

An hour later, as she dressed, Claire called Clavel to ask if he could meet with her and Jersey at 3:00.

"Where are you?" asked Clavel. "You sound far off."

"I'm at home. I'm using the speakerphone."

Once again, Clavel found himself baffled at "new" technology. Speakerphones had been around for years, but he still couldn't see the point unless you were in a conference. Multitasking was not something he did.

"That's fine. You've told Jersey?"

"I have," said Claire, winking at Jersey, who was still lying on the bed watching her dress.

"COLLEAGUES, REMEMBER," SAID CLAIRE as she and Jersey entered the police headquarters.

"Yes, Officer Simon."

"I think we should arrive separately. You go in. I'll stop by my office first to see if I have any messages and come in a few minutes."

Mme Pinan greeted Jersey with a big smile and told him to go right in, that he was expected. Thanking her, Jersey regretted he had forgotten to bring flowers and made a mental note to do so on his next visit.

He found Clavel at his desk, reading what looked to be a letter. "Come in, come in," Clavel said, pushing the letter aside and pointing to one of the two chairs in front of his desk. Before either could speak, Claire came in and took the other chair.

Clavel nodded to both Jersey and Claire, paused, took a deep breath, and gave the short speech he had prepared. He wanted to establish the ground rules for Jersey's involvement to make it clear that, while he welcomed Jersey's assistance, the investigation was and would continue to be directed by the police. They would share information with him on an "as needed" basis, and he was to keep them informed of his activities. In no case was he to represent himself as working on behalf of the police.

Claire nodded. She had expected exactly such a speech and

regretted not having warned Jersey. She could see he was angry.

Clavel smiled at Claire and looked at Jersey for his response.

Jersey avoided looking at Claire and spoke directly to Clavel. "I hope I can be of help. I understand perfectly that this is your investigation, and I would never presume to present myself as a member of your force."

Clavel merely nodded.

"But," Jersey continued, "I don't think I can help if you don't share information with me."

"I did not say we would not share information with you," said Clavel. "You will have access to all the information you need."

"But you think there is information that I won't need?"

"There may be," said Clavel in a tone indicating that that his was the final word.

"Of course," said Claire, cutting Jersey off before he could respond. Arguing with Clavel was pointless and counterproductive. She had to make Jersey understand that, together, they could work around any restrictions the "as needed" qualifier imposed. "The police sometimes obtain particularly sensitive information on condition that it not be shared outside a limited group of people. Even some police officers might not be informed. If this were to occur in this case, obviously you would not be given the information."

"Fine," said Jersey, thinking it was not at all fine but knowing from Claire's expression that it was the appropriate response.

Watching Claire and Jersey, it had become apparent to Clavel that there was more to their relationship than they let on. That didn't bother him. In fact, he was rather pleased. He was old-fashioned enough to think a woman should marry, and Jersey wasn't a bad catch. As far as the case went, he trusted Claire to respect his orders regarding Jersey's participation. And he trusted Jersey not to push her too hard.

"Where do we go from here?" asked Claire.

"Perhaps I should tell you about what I have discovered, and then you can tell me what information you think I need to follow up," answered Jersey, stressing the word need.

Two hours later, it had been decided that Jersey and Claire would go back to the Valon Gallery to examine and photograph the van Dongen the gallery claimed to have just reframed. The photo would be shown to M. Lafitte and the other van Dongen experts who later might be asked to go look at the original.

While they were at the gallery, Clavel would pay a visit to Lotan. He intended to use the tobacco leaves to get him to admit he had been in David's apartment, and to explain why. He also hoped to find out what he had been doing when Micole ran into him on the landing.

What they did after that would depend on what they found out.

Clavel hadn't mentioned the letter he had received that morning because it wasn't something he thought Jersey "needed" to know. Not yet, anyway. It was short and unsigned: *She's not what she appears to be.* He normally ignored anonymous tips, but, for some reason he couldn't put his finger on, he thought this one might be important.

CHAPTER 30

THE MORNING AFTER CLAIRE ANNOUNCED that they were to go to the Opéra Comique, Jersey set out to find a nearby restaurant to which he could take her before the show. He knew she would suggest they eat at home, which made sense given that the opera started at 8:00 and most restaurants, at least those that did not cater to tourists, began their dinner service at 7:30. But for him theater had always been associated with "dinner out."

He expected to find numerous restaurants on the place Boieldieu but found none. The neo-baroque opera house occupied one entire side of the Place. An auction house, the ticket office, and a hotel occupied the other sides. The hotel receptionist suggested the Bistrot de l'Opéra Comique or Noces de Jeannette around the corner on rue Favart. Neither menu was enticing. He was about to go back to the hotel to ask for additional suggestions when he remembered the overly long puff piece he had read in the *International New York Times* about the rue des Martyrs. According to the author, it was the "in place" to shop and dine.

Turning on the rue Lafitte, he was met by one of the most spectacular views he had seen in Paris. At the end of the street was the neo-classical church Notre-Dame-de-Lorette, and seemingly perched on its spire was the Sacre Coeur Basilica. Why, he wondered, hadn't the *Times* article even mentioned this sight? No student of his would have failed to explore a bit beyond the street that was the center of the article. He decided he'd write a letter to the editor.

Composing the letter in his head, he continued in the direction of the church. He passed a few cafés and then to his right saw the sign *Au Petit Riche*. He hesitated, trying to remember where he had heard the name. Then he remembered. It was the place of the famous food-seduction scene in de Maupassant's *Bel Ami*. The idea of dining there with Claire appealed to him. He was pleased to see that they opened for dinner at 7:00 and made a reservation. In the window there was a blurb from a guidebook that noted that the place was frequented by auctioneers and art collectors from Drouot. Maybe this wasn't such a great choice. The last thing he wanted was for this to be a working dinner. Then again, if they happened to uncover useful information, it would boost his credentials as a valuable member of the investigative team.

In their last meeting, Clavel had made it clear that he intended Jersey to play an investigative role limited initially to the operation of the Valon art gallery. Even so, Jersey saw no reason why he could not nose around elsewhere. If he uncovered something, Clavel would be hard-pressed to object, and if he found nothing Clavel would never know.

Before this trip, he had never heard of Drouot. Having been told only that it was where David had attended an auction, he expected to find a venue similar to Christie's or Sotheby's where wealthy collectors carefully examined art displayed in lavish settings and experts in bespoke suits stood ready to answer their questions. When he entered the lobby, he wondered for a minute if he was in the wrong place. The hall was noisy and crowded. The people for the most part were wearing casual, often wrinkled, shirts and thick-soled shoes. Several smoked cigars. Many seemed to be regulars, addressing the guards and each other with the familiar "*tu*."

Glancing up, Jersey noticed an illuminated sign with a list of the week's auctions. That day, there were four auctions and five pre-sale exhibits. Under the sign was a long desk behind which were seated three young women wearing Drouot badges. Like receptionists everywhere, they were "pretty" in a magazine cover sort of way. He was a bit taken aback when his question as to the location of the auctions was answered with *bonjour*. Then he remembered—why he kept forgetting was unclear—that in France it was absolutely obligatory to preface any question with *bonjour*, and that the personnel were never hesitant about providing a lesson in manners. He took a breath, smiled, said *bonjour,* and repeated the question. He was told that all of the day's auctions were on the second floor. Turning toward the escalator, Jersey spotted a familiar face walking rapidly toward the exit. It was the young man with whom he had spoken at the Valon Gallery.

Not quite believing his luck, Jersey pushed through the crowd, anxious not to lose sight of his prey. The man, to whom Jersey assigned the name Mr. V., crossed the street and entered the Café Drouot. Jersey waited a minute before following him in. Mr. V. was standing at the bar with his back to the door, talking to another man. Their faces were reflected in the mirror, and Jersey was struck by the contrast. Mr. V. had a long, pale face, small colorless eyes, and short blond hair, whereas his companion was swarthy, and had large, dark eyes and thick, curly black hair. He couldn't hear what they were saying, but by their expressions he guessed they were arguing, and that Mr. V. was on the defensive. Jersey took a place at the far end of the bar, where he hoped he would not be noticed. The two continued to talk, becoming more and more animated, when suddenly Mr. V. gulped down his drink and left. The companion seemed startled but merely shrugged and asked for the bill. Jersey paid his own bill and followed the curly-haired man into the Drouot-Richelieu Métro station. Turning the corner onto the platform, Jersey saw the train pull out. The platform was empty.

CHAPTER 31

A CCORDING TO THE MENU, AU PETIT RICHE specialized in Cuisine Lyonnaise. Which, Claire explained,
meant they should order *quenelles de brochet*.

Gefilte fish, thought Jersey with horror, on hearing the description.

"Trust me," said Claire on seeing his expression.

"OK, but it doesn't sound very seductive," replied Jersey,
wondering if she would catch the reference to *Bel Ami*.

"It's more so than anything they might have served at
Maupassant's Café Riche," she said with a wink, emphasizing
the word *Café*.

"You mean this isn't—"

"No, but Au Petit Riche has benefited from the confusion."

"How embarrassing," said Jersey, feeling truly embarrassed.

"Not at all, it's a common mistake—one they encourage."

"I'm in your hands for the rest of this meal," said Jersey,
closing his menu.

"Two *quenelles de brochet* and a bottle of Muscadet-Coteaux de la Loire," Claire told the hovering waiter, adding that they had theater tickets and would have to leave in forty-five minutes.

"I think I may have uncovered some important information," said Jersey when the waiter had left.

"Can it wait? This wasn't supposed to be a working dinner."

"I'll be brief," said Jersey before describing in considerable detail his encounters at Drouot and Café Drouot.

"I wouldn't call that brief, but I agree it could be important. Especially if the mysterious swarthy man was who I think he was."

"Who?"

"Later. When we get home, I'll show you a photo. Now let's enjoy our *quenelles*."

"Scrumptious." said Jersey. "Not at all like gefilte fish."

"Like what?"

"Gefilte fish. It's a traditional Jewish dish. The description would remind you of quenelles, but they're not at all similar."

"I'll have to try some."

"Trust me, don't," said Jersey with a grimace.

"That bad?"

"That bad. May I pour you some more of the excellent wine you selected?"

"Please. And, you should signal for the check, the opera starts in ten minutes."

During intermission, Claire gave Jersey a tour of the building. Jersey reflected that U.S. guidebooks almost always called it "a jewel," and in this case he thought the term appropriate.

"It resembles the Opéra Garnier in miniature," he remarked as they entered "le foyer," where a bar was serving champagne and mini-sandwiches.

"I prefer these murals to those at Garnier. This one is particularly splendid," commented Claire, pointing to a pastoral scene.

As he turned to look, Jersey caught sight of a familiar-looking figure. He couldn't be absolutely sure, but the young man certainly resembled the swarthy mystery man.

"Don't you think it's admirable?" asked Claire, surprised by Jersey's silence.

"What? Oh, yes, it's lovely," replied Jersey, "but take a look at that man at the end of the bar."

"Oh!" exclaimed Claire.

"Do you know him?"

"Yes, it's Olivier," said Claire, raising her program to hide her face and moving swiftly out of the foyer, thankful that the bell was ringing to signal that Act II was about to begin.

CHAPTER 32

ON MONDAY MORNING, CLAVEL RECEIVED the call he had been waiting for. The doctors at the hospital said he could now talk to David.

All hospitals, thought Clavel as he entered the reception area, are essentially alike: the same antiseptic smell, the same bland, cheery pictures lining the corridor walls, the same visitors with worried expressions carrying flowers. He introduced himself to the receptionist and was to have a seat and Dr. Botlan would be with him shortly. Within minutes, a young doctor appeared, introduced himself, and offered to take Clavel to David's room. On the way, he explained that David had total amnesia but that it was possible—not likely, but possible— that if Clavel spoke to him about the assault or about his former life, it might break the veil. He himself had tried but knew too little about David to be effective.

A uniformed policeman was keeping watch in front of room 54 and rose as Clavel approached.

"Take a break, Marcel. I'll call you when I leave," instructed Clavel.

"If you need me, just ask the nurse to page me. She'll be just outside," said Dr. Botlan after introducing Clavel.

Sitting up in bed, chatting with the nurse, was a remarkably alert young man. He seemed disappointed at being interrupted. One look at the nurse told Clavel why—she was stunningly beautiful. Despite the thick, shiny black hair tied neatly under a crisp white cap, she reminded Clavel of Catherine Deneuve in the film *Belle de Jour*. After warning that David was still weak and that he should not be excited, the nurse left them alone.

David seemed genuinely eager to help, but equally genuinely unable to do so. He said he remembered nothing. Nothing about the assault, and nothing about himself.

As the doctor had suggested, Clavel described various people and events from David's past. David merely shook his head.

Feeling as defeated as David looked, Clavel thanked him and promised to come back in a few days, when the doctors thought he might remember more. It wasn't true, but he wanted to sound encouraging.

Both the nurse and the doctor were waiting in the hall. Neither was surprised at Clavel's failure to trigger any memories. After the nurse returned to David's bedside, the doctor explained that, given the particular injury David had suffered, he expected him to totally regain his memory, but that it might take weeks if not months.

"That's good to hear, although it's bad news as far as our

investigation is concerned."

"No leads?" asked the doctor.

"Suspicions aplenty but no hard evidence. Anything David could tell us would be helpful."

"I understand. I'll let you know as soon as there are any improvements. And, just between us, I'm counting on nurse Francine to speed things along. You'd be amazed how often emotions trigger memories," said the doctor with a wink.

"There did seem to be an 'emotional' bond between the two," laughed Clavel, shaking the doctor's hand.

CHAPTER 33

TODAY WAS THE DAY HE WAS TO PICK UP the overpriced bag he had ordered for his "wife." Turning the corner onto the rue Coëtlogon, Clavel saw Olivier standing in front of the shop smoking. On seeing Clavel, he threw his cigarette into the street, ignoring, as did most smokers, the law making this illegal. Clavel was tempted to remind him of the law but didn't. Instead, he smiled and said he hoped his bag was ready. Olivier confirmed that it was and ushered Clavel into the store, where the bag was prominently displayed on the counter. Clavel had to admit it was stunning.

After a cursory examination, he expressed himself pleased and asked Olivier to wrap it as a gift. Watching him do so, Clavel noticed a bracelet on his right wrist. It was silver colored and bore an inscription he couldn't make out. Intrigued, Clavel expressed admiration and asked what it said.

"Just something in Latin. I found it at a street market last year," said Olivier, pulling his sweater down to cover the bracelet. "Will Monsieur pay by credit card?" he asked, rapidly changing the subject.

Not to be put off, Clavel asked to see the bracelet, explaining that his daughter made jewelry and he thought he might suggest she try making something similar, something with an inscription. Clavel laughed to himself at the growing size of his family.

With obvious reluctance, Olivier handed Clavel the bracelet. It read *Delta Chi.*

"Interesting, thank you," said Clavel, handing the bracelet back along with his credit card.

As soon as he was out of sight of the store, Clavel pulled out his notebook and jotted down *Delta Chi???*

CHAPTER 34

TAKING ON THE ROLE OF RICH ART COLLECTORS, Jersey and Claire headed to the Eighth arrondissement. First stop, the Valon Gallery. The gallery manager welcomed Jersey with a smile and asked him and "Madame" to have a seat while he went in the back to get the painting. Claire was relieved that the manager was not someone she had previously encountered as a member of the police.

The manager reappeared with the painting and an easel on which he set it with a dramatic bow.

"Superb," said Claire, using the word she and Jersey had agreed would mean she thought it was indeed the van Dongen photographed by David in Pierre's apartment.

"I assume you have certificates attesting to its authenticity as a van Dongen?" Jersey asked.

"Absolutely," said the manager, handing him a document.

"Hmm, yes, that seems fine. Do you also have documentation as to its provenance?"

"We obtained the painting from the estate of a European

collector. We are, unfortunately, not able to provide you with his name."

"And why is that?"

"The family insists on anonymity. This is not unusual. Wealthy collectors tend to be protective of their privacy, particularly in cases where a sale may indicate some financial distress."

"Yes, I see. And do you know when and from whom this mysterious owner obtained the painting?"

"No, I'm afraid not. But Monsieur need not worry. It is a true van Dongen. You see that on the certificate."

"We don't doubt that," interrupted Claire. "Our concern is that the seller be the legitimate owner and have the right to make the sale. A friend of ours purchased a certified Braque last year and has now been informed the painting was stolen and the sale is null and void."

"Madame need have no concern. Valon is a reputable gallery, and we stand behind all our sales," replied the manager, whose confident words were undercut by the pearls of sweat that appeared on his forehead.

"Of course," replied Jersey. "We don't mean to imply otherwise. You really needn't worry, dear," he added, turning to Claire in a soft voice but one meant to be overheard. "We are very interested in the possibility of acquiring this masterpiece but would like to think about it for a day or two," he told the manager.

"Of course. If you have any questions, please feel free to call me," said the manager, handing Jersey his business card.

"Thank you, Monsieur Laforge," said Jersey, looking at the card.

Taking advantage of Laforge's focus on Jersey, Claire quickly snapped a photo of the painting. She was quite sure Laforge would have objected. For "security reasons" she never understood, most galleries prohibited the taking of photographs of their collections. And in this case, the gallery probably had an additional reason.

"What do you think?" Jersey asked as soon as they were outside the gallery.

"It certainly looks like the painting in David's photo, and the absence of any provenance documentation is suspicious. But we need to have an expert compare the two."

"I agree, but you have to admit we could be close to solving the case."

"Could be, and clos*er*, not *close*," said Claire.

"Come on, I'm sure you see the outlines of the case as clearly as I do," replied Jersey, his voice betraying a hint of annoyance.

"Yes, we're a hell of a team," said Claire, putting her arm under his. "We owe ourselves dinner at the Épicure."

"Épicure?"

"Yes, three Michelin stars and scrumptious. In fact, it's just there. Let's look at the menu in anticipation!"

"Wow, imaginative menu—prices, too," laughed Jersey.

"It's worth every euro. And we can be 'frugal' and skip dessert."

"I think I'll have sweetbreads braised in tobacco leaves. It sounds so awful it must be delicious," said Jersey.

"I've had it, and it is. If you have that, then I'll have saddle of baby lamb roasted in black seaweed and we can share."

"Deal. I gather you've eaten here before?"

"Yes, in my former life when I worked at an auction house. As one of the only females, I was often included in business lunches with wealthy clients. It was funny. We 'took them to lunch,' meaning we chose the restaurant and then billed them for the cost."

"Interesting. Law firms in the U.S. do the same thing. I wrote a story about a particular case, thinking I had a real scoop, only to be told it was common practice, and both sides were fully aware of what was going on."

"Let's move on. We have to find out if our hunch about Troubetzkoy is correct."

The door of the Troubetzkoy Gallery was locked, but visitors were instructed to ring the bell and "*patienter*."

"Why don't they say 'please wait' instead of 'please be patient'?" asked Jersey.

"Being patient is considered less onerous than waiting because it implies you are doing something of merit," Claire explained.

"So I'm supposed to feel virtuous because I'm 'being patient'? Ridiculous."

Before Claire could answer, the door was opened by a thirty-something young woman wearing a very short red knit dress that fit like a glove. Her hair, dyed red as if to match her dress, was pulled back into a long ponytail. Were it not for the red hair, one would have guessed she was Asian. This impression was strengthened by the fact that she greeted them with a slight bow.

After the obligatory exchange of bonjours, Claire explained that they were looking to buy a copy of the work of a Fauvist painter. She and Jersey had decided that asking specifically for a van Dongen might raise suspicions. They had also decided to adopt stereotypical roles: Claire the slightly flighty art-loving wife, and Jersey the down-to-earth, cautious husband concerned with financial and legal issues rather than esthetics.

"Of course. Please sit down," said the lady-in-red, pointing to the two chairs in front of a small desk in the corner of the gallery. She took the seat behind the desk and pulled out a folder. "We have several artists who specialize in Fauves. Here are pictures of some of their works," she said, handing the folder to Claire.

Among the dozen or so photos were two of works by van Dongen, both of women with large colorful hats—his most common image. There was also a landscape by André Derain that was quite similar to *the* van Dongen.

"I like all of these," said Claire, showing Jersey the two van Dongens and the Derain. "I've always fancied having a van Dongen, but I prefer landscapes to images of women."

"Perhaps van Dongen did landscapes?" said Claire, looking inquisitively across the desk.

"He did, yes. Any book on van Dongen will have photographs of his landscapes, and our artists can certainly make a replica of any one you select."

"That could be done from a photograph of the painting?" asked Jersey.

"Absolutely. They prefer to work from images on the internet because they are now available in high definition, which enables the artist to see details you can't even see by looking at the original. One of our artists says the ability to see the brush strokes and the thickness of the paint are invaluable in making a great copy. Of course, not every painting is available in high definition. If the painting you select is not, our artists can work from an ordinary photograph."

"You refer to artists, plural. Do several artists contribute to a copy?" asked Jersey.

"No. One artist is assigned to each copy. I used the plural because we have several artists working for us."

"Does the artist sign the copy?"

"Yes. We insist, so that there is no question that we are producing copies, recognized as such, and not forgeries. There is nothing illegal about our operation."

"But the signature would not be prominent, would it?" asked Claire.

"No, a casual observer, guests at your home for example, would not notice the signature. To the untrained eye, the painting would appear to be an original, but any expert involved in a future sale would know immediately."

"Perfect," said Claire. "Once we select the painting, how long would it take to make the copy?"

"It would obviously depend on the painting. You would

discuss this with the artist."

"I'm sure the price varies as well. Is that also negotiated with the artist?" asked Jersey.

"No, you negotiate that with the gallery. Your contract would be with the gallery not the artist."

"But we could select the artist?"

"Generally the gallery selects the artist based on the painting concerned."

"So once we decide on the painting, we negotiate a price with you, you select the artist, and we then discuss the timing with him, or her. Is that correct?"

"Him. All our artists are male, unfortunately. And yes, that is the scenario."

"We're jumping ahead here," said Jersey, turning to Claire. "Could you provide us with a price range? For example, how much did the buyer pay for *this* copy?" asked Jersey, pointing to one of the photos of a van Dongen reproduction in the gallery's folder.

"That one was five thousand euros. The Derain landscape you liked was only four thousand."

"Certainly more affordable than an original. Well, thank you for your time. We will think this over and be back to you within the week," said Jersey, rising to leave.

"If you have any further questions, please give me a call," said the lady-in-red, handing Jersey a business card.

"Korean," thought Jersey, looking at the name—Dahee Lee, the same last name as his high school English teacher, who had told him Lee meant plum tree.

Out on the street, Jersey looked at Claire, cocked his head, and raised his eyebrows inquisitively.

"OK, yes, I think we're getting close," said Claire, laughing.

CHAPTER 35

AND WHAT DO YOU CONCLUDE?" ASKED CLAVEL after hearing Claire's account of their gallery visits. "I, we, think that between the time David bought the apartment and the auction, the picture of interest was removed and replaced with a copy."

"And that David discovered the switch after he purchased the copy at the auction," continued Jersey.

"And that the culprits broke into David's apartment with the intention of silencing him and destroying any evidence?" Clavel concluded.

"Exactly."

"How do you explain the timing of the theft? Why didn't the thieves steal the painting years ago?" asked Clavel.

Claire had been waiting for this question. She had wondered the same thing when discussing the case with Jersey on the walk back from the gallery. But after thinking back on everything they had learned so far, she thought she had the answer and with it the solution to the case.

"Until Pierre sold his apartment *en viager*, few people even knew the collection existed, and those who did considered its contents of little value. But when Pierre sold the apartment *en viager,* the possibility of his death was obviously raised, as it is whenever an older person sells *en viager*. At that point the value of the collection became a matter of interest to those who stood to inherit—i.e., Olivier and his sister."

"But why steal it if they were going to inherit it anyway?" asked Clavel, not because he didn't know the answer but because he wanted Claire and the rest of his team to learn to think things through before jumping to conclusions.

"Because the proceeds of the auction provided for in Irene's will would be divided between Olivier and his sister," Jersey said.

"But if it were *not* sold as part of the inheritance but on its own," continued Claire.

"Olivier would be the sole beneficiary," concluded Jersey.

"We're quite a duo," laughed Claire.

"Indeed," smiled Clavel,"but this happy story assumes, one, that Olivier knew this particular painting was valuable, and we have no evidence he was an art expert. And two, that he knew people in the art underworld who could arrange for the production of the copy and the sale of the original—again, something for which we have no evidence. And more importantly, it ignores the fact that the value of the art was also of interest to art thieves, who, like Olivier, might have focused on the collection and its value once the possibility of its being sold was raised."

"But who other than Olivier would even know the collection existed? In any case, I think I can get evidence implicating Olivier," said Claire.

"Yes?" asked Clavel, waiting for elaboration.

"Give me a day or so," answered Claire.

Clavel knew better than to insist. And, in "a day or so," he might have evidence backing his own, very different, theory of the case.

CHAPTER 36

WAITING FOR MME LANGEL TO ANSWER his ring, Clavel confirmed that, in one pocket, he had the photo Claire had taken at the Valon Gallery of the newly framed van Dongen, and, in the other, the box of tobacco he had purchased at the This is a Pipe tobacco shop.

With his waist and heart in mind, Clavel climbed the stairs to the doctor's apartment. He was just catching his breath when the door opened.

"Staying healthy, I see," remarked the doctor, more with a smirk than a smile.

"Trying, but smoking doesn't help, and thanks to you I've been indulging," replied Clavel.

"Thanks to me?"

"Yes. I visited your tobacconnist, and he introduced me to several new brands. This is the brand he said you favored," said Clavel, handing the box to the doctor.

"Thank you. It is excellent, but you didn't have to," the doctor replied, taking the box.

Clavel was pleased to have the doctor unwittingly confirm that he smoked the brand. In that case, he had to be the source of the leaves in David's apartment. The question now was, why he had been there, and why he had denied it?

"It's just a small token of my appreciation for your advice on my art investments," said Clavel, removing his coat to indicate that he intended to stay a while.

"Did you find something?"

"I saw several things, and I was hoping you would give me some additional advice," said Clavel, moving into the living room and installing himself comfortably on the sofa.

After hesitating for a moment, the doctor followed him and sat in the swivel chair facing the sofa. After his first visit, Clavel had done some research and now knew that the chair was an example of the famous, and expensive, Egg Chair designed by Arne Jacobsen. The man had money, no doubt about it. Paris was full of rich people, but for some reason the doctor's very considerable wealth troubled Clavel. Something didn't fit.

"Here is a photo of the piece I liked the best," said Clavel, taking the photo from his pocket and handing it to the doctor.

The doctor immediately rotated the chair so his back was to Clavel but not before Clavel noted his expression. The man was clearly surprised and, more than that, horrified.

"You have excellent taste," said the doctor, turning back to Clavel. "Where did you see this?"

"At the Valon Gallery. Do you know it?"

"Yes. It is a well-known gallery."

"Ah, good. I wondered because it was not among the galleries you recommended."

"No? How stupid of me," replied the doctor, shifting uneasily in his chair. "But no harm done, since you discovered it on your own."

"They claim the painting is a van Dongen."

"What price are they asking?" inquired the doctor.

"Three hundred eighty thousand euros."

"It looks to be an excellent painting, but that price is too high, even for a van Dongen. My advice would be to keep looking. You will find other works you like just as much at better prices."

"Thank you, Doctor. I'll do just that. Of course, that means I will keep bothering you for advice," laughed Clavel, rising to leave.

Back at his desk, Clavel wrote a "memo to self," as was his custom when he wanted to convince himself he was on the right track. It all fit. The final test of his theory would be whether the painting was still for sale at the Valon Gallery the next day. His guess was it would have been sold.

CHAPTER 37

YOU SOUNDED AWFULLY CONFIDENT that you could find evidence of your—no, our—theory of the case," said Jersey as they walked back to Claire's office.

"I am. And you're going to help."

"At your service," replied Jersey, taking a dramatic bow.

"I want you to go back to the Troubetzkoy Gallery and find out who among their artists replicates van Dongens."

"But Madame Lee—that's her name by the way, Ms Plum Tree—said the gallery would select the artist once we chose the painting."

"Correct. And I've chosen one," said Claire, handing Jersey a photo of a van Dongen landscape. "I'm sure, with your charm, you can get her to reveal a name, or better yet introduce you to the artist."

"I'm flattered you think so, although she didn't seem like the type who would be susceptible to my charm."

"She will be. Trust my feminine intuition. And while you're

flirting with Plum Tree, I'm going to flirt with Olivier," said Claire with a wink.

As she reached for the phone to call Olivier, it rang.

"Claire—Clavel here. I want you to ask Jersey to go back to the Valon Gallery and ask to have another look at the painting."

"And what should he look for?"

"Nothing, because I'm quite sure the painting won't be there."

"You think they suspect they've been found out? We've been very careful to hide the fact that we are with the police," said Claire, worried that she was somehow at fault.

"I'm sure you have. But I think Lotan alerted them."

"The doctor?"

"I'll explain later. Just go back today and let me know," replied Clavel. "Wait—another thing. Do you know what the words 'Delta Chi' mean?"

"Sorry, no. I suppose it's Latin, but I failed that class," laughed Claire. "Why do you ask?"

"Because Olivier wears a bracelet with that inscription."

"I'll do some research and maybe I can find a way to ask him. I'm hoping to meet him tonight."

"Good, and please let me know about the painting as soon as possible."

"Of course," said Claire, and hung up.

"Hey, Jersey, do you know what 'Delta Chi' means?" asked Claire, looking around to see where he had gone.

"It's the name of a U.S. fraternity," Jersey replied, emerging from the kitchen, munching an apple. "Why?"

"Because Clavel met Olivier this morning and he was wearing a bracelet with that inscription."

"I think I know where he got the bracelet, and I think it's part of the evidence we need to implicate Olivier," said Jersey with a huge smile. "You might not need to have a date with him."

"The man's jealous," said Claire, returning his smile.

"Maybe, but I'm serious. I'll need to check, but my hunch is that David was a member of Delta Chi. In which case the bracelet was certainly his."

"Meaning Olivier stole it?"

"Unless David gave it to him, which I doubt."

"But if he stole it, would he be foolish enough to wear it?"

"From the reports I've read, criminals are often caught because of some small thoughtless act."

"True. But at best it's evidence that Olivier's a petty thief. It's not even proof he was in the apartment, let alone in conjunction with the crime. I think my date tonight is more necessary than ever," said Claire reaching for the phone and dialing Olivier's cell phone.

CHAPTER 38

THE VALON GALLERY WAS EMPTY when Jersey entered, but no sooner had he said "Allô" than M. Laforge appeared from the back. His expression on seeing Jersey told him everything he needed to know. Clearly, this was a meeting Laforge would rather have avoided.

"Bonjour, may I be of assistance?"

"Bonjour, I've come back for another look at the van Dongen," replied Jersey, ignoring the pretense that he had not been recognized.

"Ah, yes. I'm so sorry, but the painting has been sold."

"Sold? I thought we had agreed that you would hold it for me."

"No, I regret there has been a misunderstanding, but the gallery never holds paintings without a fifty percent deposit."

"Misunderstanding? Dishonesty is a better term. I was told this was a reputable gallery, which is clearly not the case. I'll have to alert those who recommended you," said Jersey as he left, slamming the gallery door.

"Mission number one accomplished," thought Jersey as he headed to the Troubetzkoy Gallery.

He had decided that, despite Claire's suggestion that he play Don Juan, he was more likely to get the information he wanted with a businesslike approach.

Showing Mme Lee the photo Claire had given him, he asked if it would be possible to have a copy made and at what price.

"It is certainly possible. I'll have to discuss the price with the artist."

"I suggest we meet with him together," said Jersey in a firm tone meant to convey that this was a demand, not a mere suggestion.

"As I told you, the price is not something the artist negotiates with the buyer," replied Mme Lee in an equally firm tone.

"You did, but I will not commit to a purchase without having first met the artist," said Jersey, quite enjoying the role of tough businessman.

"Well, I'll have to call and ask the gallery's owner. Please wait here," she said, going into what Jersey supposed was an office at the back of the gallery.

Jersey was quite sure she would concede, but was nevertheless relieved when she returned and announced that the gallery would make a special exception in this case. They agreed that Jersey would come back the next day at 10:00 a.m. to meet the artist.

"Mission number two accomplished," thought Jersey.

CHAPTER 39

WHEN JERSEY ENTERED THE TROUBETZKOY GALLERY the next day, he was delighted to see a man meeting the description Claire had given him of Allard chatting with Mme Lee. It was the same person he had spotted days before in front of the Valon Gallery and entering the then-closed Troubetzkoy Gallery. And he was amused to note that Allard had dressed the part—a French painter as featured in American films: white smock over black jeans, red scarf knotted at the neck, and even a beret topping his glossy black hair. But rather than a paintbrush, he was holding a manila folder.

After discussing pricing and timing, Jersey left with the manila folder, which contained photos of five copies Allard had done of paintings by Fauve artists. One was of a van Dongen but, unsurprisingly, not *the* van Dongen.

He had half an hour before he was to meet Claire at the nearby Caffe Latte, so Jersey decided to make a slight detour into the Parc Monceau. He headed toward the mini flowering mountain in the center. He found it to be one of the most beautiful places in Paris and wondered, not for the first time, why it wasn't featured in every tourist book of the city. Pages were devoted to the neighboring Cernuschi and Nissim de Camondo Museums, but not a word for this magnificent structure. As he looked for an empty bench from which he could contemplate his "magical mountain," he caught sight of the backs of two women strolling down the central path. There was no mistaking the taller of the two. No one walked the way Claire did. She seemed to bounce with each step. He was tempted to go and meet them but concluded that, if it was a discussion in which Claire wanted his participation, she would have arranged to include him, and she hadn't. He didn't see any empty benches, so he continued his walk around the park, in the opposite direction of Claire and her companion.

Claire had spotted Jersey when he entered the park and had purposefully turned in the opposite direction. She did not want him to join them. Her companion was Micole, and the topic was David. If she were to solve this case, she needed to know more about the victim. More about his personality, his likes and dislikes, his dreams—things neither Jersey nor M. Lafitte would know. And Claire thought Micole was more likely to discuss David openly in a one-on-one conversation in a casual setting.

CHAPTER 40

W HAT HAVE YOU THERE?" ASKED CLAIRE, taking a seat across from Jersey at the Caffe Latte.

"Photos of works by the Troubetzkoy artist selected to work for us," said Jersey, handing her the portfolio of Allard's photos. "And guess who he is?"

"From your smile I assume it's Allard."

Jersey merely nodded.

"These are photos of copies he has done in the past?" Claire asked, hardly believing her eyes.

"So he claims. Why so astonished?"

"I need to check, but I think some of the copies are hanging on Madame Langel's walls."

"The *gardienne* of David's building?"

Claire nodded.

"Wow."

"I'll second that," said Claire before turning to the hovering waiter and ordering two cappuccinos.

"And how was your morning?"

"Useful, but nothing compared to yours. After talking with Micole, I have a clearer picture of David and one which makes me think we may be on somewhat the wrong track."

"Even after what I learned?"

"I said *somewhat*. I don't doubt that a painting was stolen and copied, or that Allard is involved. I just think there may be something much bigger than that. According to Micole, while David talked about wanting to win a Pulitzer Prize, what was more important to him, and what he didn't talk about openly, was his conviction that political corruption and criminal networks were existential threats to democratic societies."

"That sounds very dramatic and a bit juvenile. And I never heard him speak in those terms."

"As I said, she said he didn't talk about it openly. The very reason I wanted to talk to her is because I thought she would know things about him you might not. Anyway, she said that as early as high school David had argued that only journalists were in a position to bring these networks down."

"If she's correct, it means David may have been onto something bigger than one theft. And that would change the profile of those interested in silencing him."

"Exactly. And she also told me that David sold his Delta Chi bracelet to the owner of a stand at a flea market."

"Did she say why? It sounds like an odd thing to do."

"Apparently she didn't like fraternities and asked him to not wear it. She seemed quite pleased that he had gone as far as to get rid of it."

"I should hope so. Men who join fraternities typically remain committed, and if David wore a bracelet, he was among them. Selling it was a sign of true love."

"You Americans!" laughed Claire, shaking her head. "In any case it means that Olivier was telling the truth about where he got the bracelet."

"Let's go for a walk. My brain needs time to unscramble all this new information."

"I agree. First let me call Clavel and set up a meeting for tomorrow."

CHAPTER 41

C LAVEL'S REACTION TO HER AND JERSEY'S recent findings surprised Claire. She had expected him to be impressed, to offer congratulations. Instead he merely said it confirmed his thinking about the case. He promised to elaborate, but only after he had spoken with the Desrobert firm, the law firm Micole had mentioned to David as specializing in art crimes.

Judging by their offices, art crime cases were a lucrative business. The firm occupied the second floor of a nineteenth-century mansion located on the prestigious rue d'Assas near the Luxembourg gardens. The interior design was anything but nineteenth century. The reception area reminded Clavel of a showroom at Knoll—all chrome, glass, and black leather. The office into which he was shown by a young woman—who looked exactly as you would expect a receptionist at a prestigious firm to look—was similarly furnished. And the occupant of the office, Julien Desrobert, was also right out of central casting—tall, well built, with classic features, short black hair, gray suit with a pink shirt and a pink-and-gray tie, and, of course, polished black loafers. Seeing himself reflected in the glass of one of the many pictures lining the walls, Clavel chuckled to think that a snapshot of the scene would have been perfect for a "What's wrong with this picture?" game, the answer being "Clavel." In his wrinkled off-the-rack suit and dusty walking shoes, he was certainly out of place.

"Come in, Commissaire. Please have a seat."

"Thank you. Let me get straight to the point. We are investigating the vicious assault of David Barber, a young American who—we are told—may have contacted you not long before he was attacked. We have reason to suspect that the motive of the crime may relate to an investigation Monsieur Barber was conducting, and that he may have spoken with you about his work."

"Yes, he did call me, but he didn't mention an investigation. In fact, he said he was writing a novel about art crimes and wanted to know if I knew of actual cases in which thieves replaced stolen works with fakes in an effort to cover up the crime. He seemed concerned that his novel be true to life. I told him I was sure there were many such cases, but that personally I had only worked with three clients whose paintings were stolen and replaced with fakes—most recently last year. After I described the cases, he said he'd like to know more and asked if he could come and meet with me, even insisting that he would pay my hourly rate," chuckled Desrobert, adding that he doubted the young man could afford his rates.

"Did he say specifically why he wanted to meet?"

"No. I promised to have my assistant send him a report describing the cases and told him he should call me if he had further questions after reading it."

"Did he call you?"

"No."

"Tell me about the cases."

"I can give you a copy of the report we sent Barber."

"Thank you, but I'd like you to describe them briefly to me first."

"Well, the most recent case involved the theft in Geneva of an oil by Chagall from the home of a wealthy Swiss family. The family had been away on a ski holiday, and when they came home, the wife noticed something odd about the Chagall. She said it 'just didn't look right.' They took it to an expert who confirmed it was a fake. We located the original at a Parisian gallery's stand at Art Basel last year—the annual art fair in Basel. The gallery claimed it had purchased the work from a Parisian collector who had provided the necessary provenance papers. Those papers turned out to be fakes—forgeries, if you will. The gallery agreed to return the painting to the client, and the matter was dropped."

"You didn't try to identify the thief or verify if the gallery was complicit?" asked Clavel, wondering how many crimes were "settled" rather than reported.

"No. I work for private clients and only investigate what clients ask and pay me to investigate. I would be out of business immediately if I ever alerted the police against the wishes of a client. Which is why I won't tell you the identity of any of my clients."

"I understand. I find it regrettable, but I understand."

"Good. The second case involved a Modigliani etching. It was stolen from the Paris offices of a boutique law firm specializing in trusts and estates. It had acquired the original from a client several decades ago in partial payment for their services. By the way, this is not uncommon nor illegal, so long as the firm includes the value of the work as income for tax purposes, which the firm had done. Interestingly, it was the firm's scrupulousness about taxes that led to the discovery of the theft. When the government began to debate the possible imposition of a wealth tax, the firm had all its art re-evaluated, and this work was found to have almost no value, being a fake. The original was discovered in a London gallery. As in the previous case, the seller of the original, who has not been identified, provided the gallery with forged documentation, both about himself and the provenance of the painting. In this case, the gallery initially refused to return the painting on the grounds that it had purchased the painting in good faith and done its due diligence in verifying the authenticity of the documentation. However, they changed their mind when I told them I was prepared to take them to court and would ensure that the case was well publicized. One thing I've learned over the years is that the most valuable asset of upscale art galleries is their reputation, and being sued for selling a forgery, even if they prevail, can be their death knell. That was two years ago.

"The last case involved an oil by Frida Kahlo. The work was stolen from an embassy in Paris. It had been given to the embassy by heirs of the artist shortly after her death in 1954. The theft was discovered when, during a reception in his honor, a contemporary Mexican artist noticed something odd about the painting. A subsequent examination by experts confirmed that it was a fake. Within a week, a colleague, a private investigator located in Germany, located the painting in the home of a German industrialist and art collector. He had purchased the painting from a Geneva-based gallery exhibiting at the Frieze Art Fair in London a decade ago. As you can guess, the papers of provenance turned out to be forgeries. The gallery in question no longer exists, and the owners at the time of the sale are deceased. The embassy is still in negotiations with the German industrialist over return of the painting. If the embassy should decide to go to court, our firm will certainly represent them, but I doubt that will be necessary. It's in both parties' interest to settle, both to avoid unwanted publicity and to save legal fees."

"As someone with experience in art crimes, do you think the same people were involved in all three thefts?"

"I think it likely, but we have no evidence to that effect. Certainly there is more than one, or even three, criminals specializing in art theft—but the cases, as you must certainly have noticed, have elements in common."

"Which are?" Clavel asked, wanting to see if Desrobert's opinion was similar to his own.

"The paintings are all by well-known twentieth-century artists and were sold to well-known, upscale galleries, two of which had access to art fairs, a very exclusive group. Which means the thief is something of an art expert, he knows his art and the market. And my hunch, although I have no proof, is that the Parisian and Genevese galleries were complicit."

"Why is that?"

"Because well-known, established galleries employ the best experts to vet the art they sell. They know that it takes only one mistake, one misrepresentation as to the provenance of a painting, one sale of a stolen work, to put them out of business. In each of these three cases, we were able—with not too much trouble—to show that the papers provided by the seller were forgeries. It seems odd that the galleries could not have done the same. Moreover, if a reputable gallery did want to sell a work it knew to be stolen, an art fair would be the best venue. These fairs attract wealthy individuals from around the world who don't attend just to look around. They come with the clear intention of buying and are less careful than they would be elsewhere. They tend to assume that any gallery that has passed muster with the fair's organizers must be trustworthy. Of course, while most art sold at fairs is authentic, it is also true that most forgeries and stolen art are sold at art fairs."

"Why don't you think the London gallery was complicit? They must also have experts to vet their purchases."

"Yes, but they chose to offer the painting in their London gallery, rather than at Art Basel, where they had a stand at the time the work was on sale in their gallery."

"So, if a reputable Parisian gallery were in possession of a painting it knew to be stolen, it would probably not offer it for sale in its gallery in Paris?"

"It might. It might not have plans to participate in an art fair, or it might want to sell before the next fair. For example, right now there are no art fairs. The next is several months away."

"I won't ask you for the identity of your clients, not yet anyway, but I would like the names of the three galleries."

"You'll find that information in the report."

"You said you think the thief may be the same in all three cases. What about the forger? I assume it's not the same person as masterminded the thefts."

"I think you're correct. And I doubt the same person forged the three works involved. Chagall, Modigliani, and Kahlo had very different styles, and good forgers—and these were all excellently done—tend to specialize in a particular style."

"They are all twentieth-century artists, though."

"Yes," chuckled Desrobert a bit dismissively, "but the twentieth century includes a wide variety of schools, Fauvism, Surrealism, Expressionism, Cubism, among others."

"But a forger might specialize in, say, Fauves?"

"Yes. Some specialize in one particular artist, but the Fauve style—Fauvism—is certainly something in which a forger might develop a particular expertise."

"Thank you for your time. You've been helpful. If I could have a copy of the report, I'll let you get back to work."

His next stop was Lafitte's gallery. As Clavel feared, M Lafitte declined to pass judgment on the authenticity of the van Dongen based on a photograph. He now regretted having alerted Lotan. He had thought it was a clever move but, since his suspicions had proven correct and the gallery had removed the painting, there was no way, at least for now, for Lafitte to examine the actual painting.

CHAPTER 42

BACK IN HIS OFFICE, CLAVEL SUMMONED inspectors Luc and Jean-Paul. "I want you two to set up a stake-out in front of 16 rue Cassett. If Dr. Lotan leaves, I want him followed. If he meets with anyone, I want to know with whom. Which means one of you will probably have to follow that person while the other sticks with Lotan. I doubt he'll have visitors, but, if he does, I want to know who."

"What about tonight?"

"Find two colleagues, anyone, to replace you from midnight to 6:00 a.m. But I want you two back there tomorrow. Put everything else you're doing on hold. This may take several days."

It took only two hours before Clavel received a call from Jean-Paul saying he was following Lotan, who had taken a taxi and was heading toward the Luxembourg Gardens. A few minutes later, a second call came in saying Lotan had just entered 34 rue du Cardinale LeMoine.

Olivier's apartment was the last place Clavel had expected

Lotan to go. It didn't fit with his theory of the case. Could Claire be correct? he wondered.

His thoughts were interrupted by a call from Luc saying that, on returning to 16 rue Cassett, Lotan had gone to visit Mme Langel. He was still there.

Just over an hour later, Luc reported that Lotan had returned to his own apartment.

These visits meant Clavel had to rethink his theory of the case. His thoughts were interrupted by the appearance of Claire's head in the doorway.

"Come in. I have news. Lotan just paid a visit to Olivier's apartment," declared Clavel.

"I'm not surprised. And the timing is good because I have a date with Olivier tonight. I'll use all my charm to find out about his relationship with Lotan or—let's say—to corroborate what I think," replied Claire with a smile that said "I told you so."

"Or refute," said Clavel with a wink. "And Olivier wasn't the only person Lotan visited. He spent over an hour with Langel."

"There, I'm surprised. An hour is far more time than would be needed to discuss a building-maintenance matter, and I don't picture him as the type to socialize with a *gardienne*."

"My view exactly."

"Do you think the meeting is relevant to our investigation?"

"I think it's critical," answered Clavel.

"Go on."

"We obviously need to find out what was discussed, but I think it's evidence that a wider network of people were involved in the crime—at least in the theft of the painting—than I had previously thought. Am I correct in thinking that you established a cordial relationship with Madame Langel when you last met with her?"

"I think that's right."

"Then I want you to meet with her again—use any pretext—and find out as much as you can about her relationship with Lotan."

"Maybe I should just meet with Lotan and ask about his relationship with both Olivier and Langel?" joked Claire.

"I only wish your charm was that formidable," said Clavel laughing.

"It's time for me to go home and get ready for my date. I'll brief you tomorrow morning."

"Let's say tomorrow afternoon. In the morning I want you to pay a visit to Madame Langel."

CHAPTER 43

WHEN CLAIRE ARRIVED AT THE BISTRO Au Petit Suisse, Olivier was waiting outside. "Change of plans," he said, taking Claire's arm under his. "We're going to Guy Savoy."

Claire wondered if she had heard correctly. Guy Savoy was one of the most expensive, and one of the best, restaurants in Paris.

"Yes, Guy Savoy," grinned Olivier, responding to her look of surprise. "We're celebrating my new life of leisure."

"So your mysterious plan worked out?" Claire asked, recalling their earlier conversation.

Olivier merely nodded as he hailed a taxi.

Claire quickly decided that she was likely to learn more about his new source of wealth by not asking any questions. He was so clearly eager to impress her that he wouldn't be able to stand her silence and apparent indifference.

By the time the taxi reached 11 quai de Conti, Olivier had explained that he had finally closed a deal he had been working on, adding with obvious pride that he had come up with an offer the other party couldn't refuse.

The room into which they were ushered was decorated in slate gray tones. The walls were hung with contemporary art, and the long French windows gave onto the Seine and the Louvre. A snide review might have said it "reeked" of elegance, reflected Claire.

Claire knew what she was going to order for a first course even before looking at the menu: the restaurant's renowned artichoke-and-truffle soup, accompanied by a wild mushroom-stuffed brioche. She'd ask Olivier what he recommended for a main course. He'd be flattered that she thought he had been here before.

He recommended the lobster surrounded by raviolis stuffed with shrimp—the most expensive dish on the menu. He had the same.

As was fitting, the conversation throughout the meal was about food. It turned out that Olivier was quite a gourmet. Even before he could afford to do so, he had frequented the best Parisian restaurants. His love of the good life was clearly genuine and long-standing—the perfect precursor to a life of shady deals, thought Claire.

It was only while sipping her cognac that Claire brought the conversation back to Olivier and his recent good fortune. If, as the timing suggested, Lotan was the other party in his "deal," what was the offer he had found too good to refuse? Why would Lotan pay Olivier now? It didn't fit.

"To your deal-making skills," she said, raising her glass.

"Is this the first celebration?"

"Absolutely. We closed the deal this afternoon."

"What's next?"

"I think I'll quit my job and maybe travel. I'm not sure."

"But don't you want to do other deals?"

"No. -Actually, I'm not much of a business person. This was just a lucky fluke, a once in a lifetime thing," he replied, signaling for the check.

Out on the street, Claire took his arm and suggested he walk her home, it being such a lovely evening. He laughed and said he'd be delighted to walk her home, his home. When she shook her head, his expression changed to one of surprise and anger. After staring at her for what seemed a long time, as if deciding what to do, he turned around and walked away.

"All for the best," Claire said to herself as she watched him go. "I know what I need to know, and I was becoming too fond of him."

CHAPTER 44

CLAIRE WAS GLAD JERSEY WAS ASLEEP when she got home. She knew that, if she talked about Olivier, her ambivalent feelings would be obvious, and not appreciated.

She woke to the smell of freshly brewed coffee and found Jersey in the kitchen preparing a breakfast tray of freshly baked brioches. Any ambivalence she felt last night over losing Olivier vanished. Unseen, she tiptoed back to bed and waited for him to come and wake her.

"Would sleeping beauty like some breakfast?" he asked, taking a slight bow and placing the tray on the bed.

"If my Prince Charming will join me."

"He will," said Jersey, slipping back into bed.

"Too bad I have to visit the *gardienne*," said Claire as she finished her coffee. "And I'd better hurry, because after ten she's on duty, and I don't want to be interrupted by a delivery person or a resident."

"Have you decided on an approach?"

"I think I'll continue with the approach I used during my last visit. She saw me as someone who admired her sense of style, so she seemed eager to promote herself as belonging to a higher social class than most *gardiennes*. An obvious way for her to do that would be to acknowledge she had a social relationship with a tenant."

"But if Clavel is correct that she and Lotan are co-conspirators in the Barber case, she's more likely to deny having any kind of special relationship with him, even if it would attest to her high social standing."

"Exactly."

"Clever."

CHAPTER 45

C LAIRE RANG MME LANGEL'S DOORBELL and waited. On the fifth ring, an angry voice answered. "It's only 9:00 a.m. Come back at ten."

Claire rolled her eyes and rang again. This time, as soon as she heard the click indicating Mme Langel had picked up, she said, "Police." The magic word, thought Claire, better than "open sesame."

"Good morning. I'm really sorry to bother you again, but we have a few questions I'm sure you can help us answer."

"I hope it won't take long. I had hoped to go out to do some shopping, but if you think I can help. . . ."

"Oh, I'm sure you can. As a person with a true sense of style and exquisite taste, I assume you have connections in the art world."

Mme Langel merely smiled and nodded.

"Yes, well, perhaps then you know friends of Dr. Lotan, friends from the art world? We're trying to identify people with knowledge about art who would be familiar with the building."

"Oh, no, no. I know Dr. Lotan only as a resident. I've never met him socially. We rarely speak. I didn't even know he was interested in art," said Mme Langel, wringing her hands and shaking her head.

"Do you think your son, the artist, might be able to help?"

"My son? He has never met the doctor."

"You did tell me he was an artist, and he might have met the doctor without your knowledge. I certainly don't tell my mother about all the people *I* meet," said Claire with a laugh. "In any case, I'd like to speak to him. If you give me his number, I'll be off and won't take any more of your time."

"He is very busy."

He doesn't like being disturbed. I'm really sure he doesn't know anything about the Doctor or his friends."

"Maybe not, but I'd like to speak with him. I'm sure you want us to solve this case as quickly as possible, and it would waste time if I had to get a mandate."

Mme Langel hesitated and then, without a word, handed Claire a piece of paper on which she had written *Jacques 0675520122.*

As soon as she was on the street out of sight of the building, Claire called 0675520122. The line was busy, as she had expected. She immediately dialed Mme Langel's number. It too was busy. She then called her office and asked Jean-Paul to find out to whom the number 0675520122 belonged.

CHAPTER 46

F ROM YOUR EXPRESSION I gather you have news," said Clavel as Claire and Jersey entered his office.

"You bet I do. Let me tell you about the concierge, sorry, *gardienne*, first."

When she had finished, Clavel asked why she had not mentioned that they saw Lotan go to her apartment the day before.

"I wanted to worry her, but not too much. We can give her lots of reasons to worry, but one at a time. In retrospect, I wish I hadn't brought up her son."

"I think it was brilliant," said Jersey. "You confirmed what we had only suspected—that Allard is her son."

"But now that he's been warned we're on to him, we're unlikely to get any information out of him," replied Claire.

"True, but if he is involved, he would have been alerted by Lotan or the Valon Gallery. I agree with Jersey, you did a superb job. I hope you did as well with Olivier," said Clavel with a smile.

"Better," said Claire and then launched into a detailed description of her evening.

"So you think the purpose of Lotan's visit was to pay Olivier?" asked Clavel.

"Yes, the timing leaves no doubt. If Olivier had concluded his so-called deal earlier, he would have let me know about the change of venue of our dinner before meeting me at the Petit Suisse. But what I don't understand is why Lotan would pay Olivier now, unless the painting just sold."

"Obviously, we'll have to check that. But I think you're making an unjustified assumption," said Clavel.

"Which is?"

"That the payment was Olivier's share of the painting's sale price."

"What else. . . . Wait—do you mean. . . . ?" Claire closed her eyes as if trying to conjure up a scene. Shaking her head, she continued. "How could I have been so blind? The evidence was there from the start, from that first conversation with Allard."

"I didn't catch it at the time either," said Clavel. "Only later did I get the sense Olivier hadn't played the role you ascribed to him. But it was only a hunch. I needed further substantiation, and you've just provided it."

"So what do we do now?" asked Jersey, clearly baffled.

"I want Claire to get one more bit of information, and then I think we move to the accusation stage," said Clavel with a smile.

"Well-founded accusations, even without solid proof, generally trigger confessions," Claire explained, noticing Jersey's bewildered expression.

"Claire, I want you to visit the Parisian Gallery, and the London, mentioned in Desrobert's report. We need descriptions of the person from whom they purchased the stolen paintings," said Clavel.

"Do you think they'll remember?" asked Jersey, turning to Clavel.

"A reputable high-end art gallery doesn't forget having been hoodwinked into buying a fake. If they claim not to remember, it will mean Desrobert is correct that they were complicit, and a reminder that we can hale them into court should jog their memory."

CHAPTER 47

THE PARISIAN GALLERY WAS LOCATED on rue Saint-Honoré, across the street from the Bristol hotel—an address designed to attract wealthy international buyers, many of whom undoubtedly stayed at the Bristol while in Paris. The location also attested, or at least was intended to attest, to the excellent reputation of the gallery and the quality of its collection. So, too, did the fact that you had to ring to be let in.

A middle-aged, conservatively dressed woman opened the door with a smile. Claire decided she must have practiced in front of a mirror. It was polite, slightly subservient. Claire responded with her own on-the-job smile and pulled out her police badge.

"There must be a mistake—we didn't call the police."

"I know you didn't, but we have some questions about a case in which the gallery was involved several years ago. A case involving a stolen Chagall at Art Basel."

"You must be mistaken. This gallery would never traffic in stolen art," said the woman in a firm voice she clearly hoped would put an end to the discussion.

"Not frequently or intentionally perhaps, but you did offer one for sale at the Art Basel fair three years ago. Our investigation shows that, presented with the evidence, the gallery returned the painting to the rightful owner. I can't imagine you would forget what must have been a considerable financial loss."

"Art Basel, you say? Yes, I do remember now. A most unfortunate, and as you say costly, mistake on our part."

"What puzzles me, Madame. . . ?"

"Menguy."

"What puzzles me, Madame Menguy, is why the gallery didn't go after the person who sold you the painting."

"Oh, we tried, but of course he hadn't given us his real name or address. We could have hired lawyers and detectives but decided that would just be throwing good money after bad. In this case, we decided it was best to cut our losses and learn our lesson."

"Best for you and the gallery's reputation perhaps, but not for society. Failure to report a crime is itself a crime, as I'm sure you know."

"No, no, I didn't, the gallery didn't. In fact, it was the owner's lawyer who suggested we settle between ourselves. We . . .we didn't imagine it was a crime. A lawyer wouldn't suggest it if it were a crime," stammered Mme Menguy, shifting nervously in her chair.

"It is, but we won't pursue the matter if you will help us identify the man. We have several suspects, and I'd like you to look at some photos and tell me if any of them look familiar."

Claire pulled a stack of photos out of her briefcase. They were all middle-aged men; one was Lotan. Claire laid one photo at a time on the desk. Each time, Mme Menguy merely shook her head. Claire nevertheless had the impression that she was troubled on seeing Lotan. An almost imperceptible reaction, but one she noticed.

"You're sure you don't recognize any of these men?"

"No, I don't remember ever seeing any of them before. As best I can recal,l the man was younger and heavier set than the people in your pictures."

"Interesting. Most interesting," said Claire, putting the photos back in her purse.

Rising to leave, Claire noted that the ambiguous words had had the desired effect. Mme Menguy was clearly very worried.

On her way back to the office, Claire stopped in the misnamed Square Marigny, which was actually a lovely park, not a square, to call Clavel. She wanted his advice on how to approach the London Gallery. The plan was for her to telephone them; time and budget restrictions ruled out a trip to London. The use of photos had been his idea, and a good one, but certainly wouldn't work when dealing over the phone. Even if she emailed them the photos, she wouldn't be able to judge their reactions.

"Given what you just learned, I suggest you simply ask them for a description of the person from whom they purchased the Modigliani. I think they'll cooperate, but if they show any reluctance to cooperate, let them know that we can go public with our investigation, and will. From what Desrobert told me, that will change their attitude."

"But if they are complicit, they won't provide an accurate description."

"True, but Desrobert doesn't think they were, and I trust his judgment."

Her call was answered by the deep, raspy voice of a chain smoker. It was Mr. Whitman, the long-time gallery owner. He immediately acknowledged having personally purchased the Modigliani and expressed enthusiasm at the prospect that the police might catch the crook, who he suspected was a repeat offender. He described the man as in his seventies, with white hair, tall, well built, and well groomed, with a slightly feminine appearance.

"Would you be able to identify him in a lineup?" asked Claire.

"Absolutely. What fun, right out of the movies," chuckled Mr. Whitman.

"It might require that you come to Paris."

"I'd be delighted. Oh, another thing: He claimed to be a pipe-smoker."

"Claimed to be?"

"That may not be the correct verb. Let's say he mentioned the fact when he noticed my collection of pipes."

CHAPTER 48

C LAIRE, JERSEY, AND MME PINAN WAITED patiently as Clavel arranged his notes on the conference table. "We have reams of evidence that I think we all agree point to the involvement of four individuals—Allard, Langel, Lotan, and Olivier," he said, pointing to the notes.

"Are you implying Allard is the leader?" questioned Jersey.

"No, the order in which I listed the names is merely alphabetical. But you raise a key issue, and that is what role each of these people played. The evidence suggests—I stress *suggests*— that we have two related but separate crimes. First the theft of a van Dongen, and second the vandalism of the apartment and attack on David."

"Isn't it really one crime—the vandalism was clearly designed to cover up the theft," Jersey pointed out.

"Most likely, but what is far from clear is what role our four suspects played in each, or even whether they were all involved in both incidents."

"The only way we're going to figure that out is if one of them turns what in the U.S. we call state's-evidence," continued Jersey.

"Exactly. And that is why I've called this meeting. We need to decide who that person is and how best to approach them." Looking around the table, Clavel said, "Ideas?"

"I'd suggest Olivier," said Mme Pinard.

Clavel smiled, wondering on which whodunit she was basing her suggestion.

"Claire? Jersey?"

"I'm out of my league here," demurred Jersey.

"I agree with Madame Pinan," said Claire. "Olivier knows a lotm and I think he has less to lose in the facts coming out than the others."

Clavel nodded.

"OK, I'll trust female intuition," said Clavel, nodding toward Mme Pinan and Claire. "Next question: what approach do we take?"

It took close to an hour before a plan was agreed upon.

Chapter 49

MME PINAN GREETED OLIVIER and asked him to take a seat in Clavel's office, explaining that he had been called away but would return shortly. She left the door ajar so as to have a view into the room from her desk.

She watched as Olivier looked nervously around the office and finally took a seat in front of the desk. Within seconds, he got up and moved to the sofa.

After letting him fidget for a few minutes, Clavel walked in. Olivier stood up abruptly, letting his bag fall onto the floor.

"Good morning," said Clavel curtly, taking a seat behind his desk and gesturing to the chair in front.

He pulled a folder out of the drawer and began to riffle through it, all in silence.

Olivier shifted uneasily.

Clavel closed the folder and took a deep breath. "I think you know why you're here."

"No, no, I don't," said Olivier in a voice that lacked conviction.

"You do know the apartment previously owned by your mother was broken into earlier this month, and the current owner, Monsieur Barber, was serious injured?"

"Yes, of course I've heard, and I already told one of your colleagues that I wish I had information that could help find the thugs, but I don't."

"We have evidence to the contrary. Not only do you know who was involved, but you know why. You have so much information, in fact, that Doctor Lotan paid you a considerable sum to keep that information to yourself."

"...Who?"

"Please, you do yourself no good by denying what we can prove. The only way you are going to avoid a stint in prison is by cooperating and telling us everything you know."

Noticing that Olivier was about to protest, Clavel raised his hand, cutting him off. "My colleagues think, not only that *do* you know who was involved, but that you are among them. And they are ready to bring charges, which, if proven, will land you in jail for years. There is considerable evidence to support that view. However, my own sense is that your involvement was limited to suppressing evidence. If that is so and you reveal what you know, I will recommend leniency, and you will likely only be subject to a financial penalty."

"I told you, I don't know anything about the break-in. No one would pay me a *centime* to keep quiet when I have nothing to say."

"You're correct. Doctor Lotan would not have paid you if you had nothing to sell. But we know he *did* pay you, paid you one hundred thousand euros. If you say it wasn't for your silence, what was it for?"

"That is an outrageous allegation! I only *wish* someone would give me that kind of money," said Olivier, smiling and leaning back in his chair.

Less-experienced investigators might have been misled by Olivier's easy, self-assured manner. But Clavel noticed a look of panic in his eyes. He'd seen it before when questioning suspects, suspects who ultimately were proven guilty.

Clavel opened the folder and pulled out a single piece of paper. Tapping it, he continued. "You recently deposited sixty thousand euros in your savings account at Crédit Agricole and opened new accounts at four other banks, in each of which you deposited ten thousand euros. You did this one day after Doctor Lotan paid you a visit. Which was the same day *he* withdrew one hundred thousand euros from *his* bank. I don't think this is a coincidence."

Olivier hesitated, considering his next move. Clavel looked him in the eyes and waited, another tactic perfected over the years. Suspects generally found the intense, silent scrutiny unnerving.

Olivier proved to be no exception. "OK. You're right. Lotan did pay me to keep quiet. In fact, it's rather funny, because all I had were suspicions. I didn't have any evidence, although of course I claimed I did, and they fell for it," Olivier said with a slight laugh.

"If he paid you, your suspicions were obviously well founded."

"Yeah, I thought I was pretty clever."

"Crime is rarely clever, and usually very costly. But you won't have to pay much of a price if you help us nail Lotan and the others involved."

After having been promised that Clavel would not tell Lotan or Allard that they had spoken, Olivier recounted how he had come to suspect both of stealing the van Dongen and replacing it with a copy.

During his mother's last days, she had summoned him and his sister to explain her will and urged them to have the value of the paintings determined by an independent expert not associated with the auction house before they were auctioned. She asked Olivier to select the expert only after Pierre's death. She didn't explain why she had never had them valued, or why she didn't trust the auctioneer she had selected. Olivier suspected that she may have known some of them were extremely valuable and for some reason didn't want that known so long as the works were in her or Pierre's possession. His sister had thought the request was absurd but told Olivier to do whatever he wanted, to just send her a check for her half after the auction. After his mother died, Olivier had decided to do his own research into the value of the collection, and to do so before Pierre died, but without his knowledge. He claimed his sole motive was curiosity. If he stood to inherit a fortune he wouldn't have to worry about incurring debt and could improve his lifestyle immediately. He couldn't imagine Pierre would live too much longer.

His first step was to photograph all the works. He had told

Pierre it was for memory's sake, as Clavel already knew. He then had three friends from his days at Beaux Arts, all of whom now worked in modern art departments of Christies and had expertise evaluating art, look at them. He told them they were from the home of his latest girlfriend, which would explain why they didn't know the "friend" and why they couldn't go look at the originals. They all singled out the work in question as a van Dongen, although they couldn't tell from just a photo if it was real or a copy. He then asked Allard, a close friend, to meet him in the apartment to look at the actual painting. He again told Pierre he wanted to take a few more pictures. Allard had examined the painting carefully and taken a number of photos. A few days later, he told Olivier he had shown the photos to experts at the gallery where he worked, all of whom said it was clearly a copy, a good copy but a copy. Olivier accepted this verdict and didn't bother to have an independent expert evaluation at the time of Pierre's death—a decision he called the stupidest one of his life.

It was only a month or so after the auction that he happened to see the painting in the Valon Gallery, priced at €360,000. He knew it was his mother's painting because of the scratch in the top corner. The gallery said they had acquired it recently from the estate of a "European collector" whose name they couldn't disclose. They didn't need to. Olivier knew it was Allard. He confronted Allard and threatened to go to the police unless he was given a cut from the sales price. He figured Allard had collaborators but had no idea Lotan was involved—until Lotan showed up and offered to pay him. He still didn't know what role Lotan played but guessed it was a major one. He didn't seem like a guy who would play second fiddle to Allard. He also suspected that Langel was involved. He knew she was Allard's mother and the timing of her sudden unexplained good fortune couldn't be a mere coincidence. He hadn't bothered to investigate further; he had what he wanted, information worth a good deal of money. Bringing criminals to justice wasn't his job.

"I find your selfish nonchalance abhorrent, but I will recommend leniency if your information contributes to the conviction of Lotan and company and we don't find evidence that you played a role in the actual theft or break-in. You're free to go, but don't leave Paris," Clavel concluded, signaling that Olivier could leave.

"And you won't let Allard or Lotan know I spoke to you?"

"No, nor will any of my colleagues."

CHAPTER 50

MME PINAN GREETED MME LANGEL and asked her to take a seat in Clavel's office, explaining that he had been called away but would return shortly. She left the door ajar so as to have a view into the room from her desk.

She watched as Mme Langel looked nervously around the office and finally took a seat in front of the desk. Within seconds, she got up and moved to the sofa.

After letting her fidget for a few minutes, Clavel walked in. She stood up abruptly, letting her purse fall onto the floor.

"Good morning," said Clavel curtly, taking a seat behind his desk and gesturing to the chair in front.

He pulled a folder out of the drawer and began to riffle through it, all in silence.

Mme Langel shifted uneasily, crossing and uncrossing her legs.

Clavel closed the folder and took a deep breath. "I think you know why you're here, Madame Langel."

"No, no, I don't," said Mme Langel in a voice that lacked conviction.

"Then I'll tell you. We know that you and your son were involved in the theft of the van Dongen from the Marens' apartment, and my colleagues think also in the assault on Monsieur Barber. These are serious crimes that could put you both in prison for a very long time—for life if Monsieur Barber dies."

"It's not true, my—"

"Let me finish. We suspect that others were also involved, but we need more evidence, and I think you can provide it. If you do, I will recommend leniency for you in exchange for your help."

One look at Mme Langel convinced Clavel that he had chosen the perfect strategy. The look of fear had disappeared, replaced by a look of relief.

"What about my son?"

"If you tell us what we need to know to convict the leaders of this operation, I will recommend leniency for him also."

Mme Langel took a tissue out of her purse, wiped the sweat from her forehead, and leaned forward. Just as she seemed about to speak, Clavel raised his hand and warned her that any attempt to mislead the police or hide the truth would be her and her son's ticket straight to jail.

Claire and Mme Pinan, who had followed the conversation from the outer office, shook hands in mutual self-congratulation.

CHAPTER 51

THE STORY TOLD BY MME LANGEL WAS NOT the story Clavel or his team had expected. It confirmed what they suspected and filled in some gaps, providing them with the ammunition they needed to go after the doctor and put him behind bars for decades. But it also revealed that Mme Langel was not the bit player they had thought. Even with leniency, she too would face years in jail. As would Allard. Only Olivier was likely to escape with a mere fine. For which Claire admitted to herself she was glad.

After dismissing Mme Langel with the warning not to leave Paris and to remain available, Clavel gave a copy of the deposition to Claire and asked her to read it over carefully. They would meet the next morning to decide the next and final steps.

"So?" asked Jersey the moment Claire entered the apartment.

"*Bonsoir*," said Claire with a smile.

"Sorry, I forgot. *Bonsoir*. Now tell me," laughed Jersey.

"A drink first. I fancy a Black Russian—two parts vodka

one part Kahlua," said Claire, thinking of her first date with Olivier.

"Interesting choice."

"Hmm. You should try one, too."

Sipping her drink, Claire summarized the deposition for Jersey.

"So Langel actually instigated the theft. I clearly misjudged her. How did Clavel get her to admit it?"

"The way he always does, by painting a picture of what he thought had happened in which she played a larger, more nefarious role than he actually thought she had. It's rare that a suspect resists the urge to correct him and in doing so inevitably tells him things he didn't know. In this case he accused her, not only of stealing the painting, but of masterminding the break-in and attack on David, who, he implied, could die—making her guilty of murder!"

"Phew. That would scare even the most hardened criminal. Do you think she opened the mail of all the tenants?"

"I would suppose so. I think she felt resentful at being a concierge and hoped she might find some minor embarrassing tidbit she could share with her friends, or leverage for a tip. I doubt she knew she would find evidence of criminal activity in the doctor's mail."

"I wonder how she would have used the information if Allard hadn't seen the work and told her it was a genuine van Dongen."

"She probably hadn't decided, but that discovery provided the obvious answer. Either Lotan collaborated with them to steal the painting, or she would go to the police with what she knew."

"Do you believe she came up with the plan alone and had to persuade Allard to make the copy?"

"No. I don't think Allard was the least bit reluctant. He's a bit of a dandy with a life style he can ill afford on what he earns at Troubetzkoy. And according to Madame Danine, the gallery owner, he wasn't much for an honest day's work. I do think, however, that it was her idea to insist on being paid immediately. As she said, she didn't trust Lotan to give her a fair share if she waited for the picture to sell. And she didn't want to wait."

"I assume Clavel is now going to confront Lotan?"

"Correct. And, even if he doesn't confess, we will probably have sufficient evidence to gain a conviction in court, at least for the theft of the van Dongen."

"What about the assault on David and the string of earlier thefts?"

"That will be harder. Langel claims she wasn't involved in planning the break-in, and I'm inclined to believe her. She did seem sincere when she said she was horrified that they had harmed David. She pinned the responsibility on Lotan, but I wouldn't give that much weight, given her obvious dislike of Lotan, and the fact that she has no proof."

CHAPTER 52

LAVEL HAD THOUGHT LONG AND HARD about how best to approach Lotan. He was convinced Lotan was involved, not only in the Barber case, but also in Desrobert's three cases, and probably a host of other thefts as part of an organized art mafia. But he still didn't have sufficient proof to ensure conviction. Lotan was not likely to confess, and if accused he would plead innocent and hire a good defense attorney. Clavel needed Lotan to incriminate himself. The man was too clever to do that under questioning from the police. And he wasn't the type to be seduced by Claire, even in the unlikely event that he didn't suspect her of being a cop. There was just one person who might be able to get Lotan to let down his guard and speak a bit too freely.

When he explained his plan to the team, Claire shook her head and rolled her eyes, implying she thought Clavel was out his mind. To her it was clear that the person he had in mind would work with Lotan to mislead the police, not the other way around. Luc and Jean-Paul approved, as they always did.

Clavel couldn't remember a time they had disagreed with him. Mme Pinan nodded and proclaimed Clavel's idea brilliant, saying it was just what Simenon's Maigret would do. Jersey shrugged, again feeling out of his league.

"In that case, it's a go," said Clavel with a huge smile.

CHAPTER 53

'M DELIGHTED TO SEE YOU AGAIN, COMMISSAIRE. To what do I owe the pleasure?" asked Mme Corez, ushering Clavel into her living room. "I'll just make some coffee," she said before he could answer.

"Thank you, that would be lovely," said Clavel, taking a seat on the sofa. He was surprised how uneasy he felt. He liked Mme Corez and felt a certain reluctance to use her to build his case against Lotan. At the same time, he worried that he might have misjudged her, that she might be in cahoots with Lotan or at least so enamored as to be reluctant to cooperate.

"I assume this is not a purely social call," said Mme Corez as she set the coffee service down on the coffee table.

"No, I'm afraid not," answered Clavel, taking a deep breath. "I'm here to ask for your help."

"As I said before, I'm eager to help in any way I can," interrupted Mme Corez.

"There is one way you can be of immense help. But it is something I suspect you will be reluctant to undertake. And you are, of course, free to refuse."

The expression on Mme Corez's face reassured Clavel. She looked puzzled, not worried, as she would have had she been involved in the crime, or known that Lotan was.

"As you know, we have been investigating the break-in of David Barber's apartment, and the assault on David, for some time. Two of those involved have confessed and implicated a third. We also have evidence backing up their stories. Our case against the third person is strong but not foolproof. I'm hoping you can help us obtain that proof."

"I'm completely baffled. I can't imagine how I could possibly help obtain evidence against someone I don't even know."

"You do know him. It's Doctor Lotan."

"*George?* That's not possible. I've known him for years. He would never do anything illegal, let alone destroy property and physically harm someone. He's a doctor. His life has been spent healing, not harming. And he liked David."

Her surprise seemed genuine, reinforcing Clavel's conviction that she was in no way involved. It wasn't clear if her apparent outrage was equally genuine. His impression was that, while she probably didn't know about his role in the break-in, she did not find the idea inconceivable. If that was the case, convincing her to help the police might not be difficult.

"You may be correct, and you can help us determine if you are. As things stand, we have sufficient credible evidence to arrest the doctor. And we will do so even if, to be honest, the evidence is not strong enough to ensure conviction. On the other hand, if he is not guilty, it would be best for all concerned if we knew that prior to making an arrest. And I think you can help us gather additional evidence to help us make that determination. I'm sure the doctor would prefer not to go through the humiliation of being arrested and tried, even if he is ultimately proven not guilty."

As Clavel spoke, Mme Corez had sat motionlessly staring at the floor. When he finished, she looked up and, as her eyes met his, she smiled slightly and nodded.

"Thank you," said Clavel, returning the smile.

The next half hour was spent discussing the role Mme Corez was to play. It was finally decided that she would tell Lotan she had been informed by the police that he was their prime suspect in the break-in and assault, and lay out for him the evidence the police said they had. She would make it very clear that she didn't care if he was involved in the break-in, implying she thought he probably was, and that she just wanted to know what she could do to help him avoid arrest.

Mme Corez laughed and said she was sure he would believe this, explaining that Lotan had a very high regard for himself and considered her his inferior and as someone he could manipulate. She seemed to consider it a good joke rather than an insult.

CHAPTER 54

AFTER RECEIVING MME COREZ'S REPORT on her discussion with Lotan, Clavel called an emergency staff meeting. "We have our case," announced Clavel when they were all seated.

"And we have Mme Corez to thank. The arrogant fool actually believed she was willing to help him cover up. He asked her to simply back up the story he planned to tell the police. The details of the story he concocted show that he knew things only a guilty person would. For example, he explained how he had never been to the Whitman Gallery in London. But she had not told him the name of the gallery, not knowing it herself. He also dismissed any testimony by Madame Langel as lacking credibility, she being a mere concierge. Yet Madame Corez had not mentioned that Langel was the source of incriminating testimony. Most amusing was that he asked her to say she was with him when he visited David's apartment shortly before the break-in, and that they had gone to discuss some items on the agenda of the upcoming annual meeting of the building's board. Again, she had not mentioned that the police suspected he had been in the apartment despite his repeated denials."

CHAPTER 55

WITHIN A WEEK, LOTAN WAS UNDER ARREST and awaiting trial for the theft of the van Dongen and earlier theft of the Modigliani. Clavel was sure he would win a conviction for both based on the testimony of Langel, Olivier, Allard, and the gallery owner, Mr. Whitman who, without hesitation, singled out Lotan in a lineup. Alone, this would send Lotan to prison for a number of years. But Clavel wanted more. He wanted a conviction for the assault on David and, for this, he lacked evidence. He didn't think Lotan had actually participated but was sure he had masterminded the operation and knew the other participants.

Olivier, Langel, and Allard all claimed to have been horrified at the assault and to know nothing about the operation, which Clavel found credible. The only solution was to persuade Lotan to identify the assailants.

It was Claire who came up with what Clavel thought the best strategy. It would require lying which, while contrary to official police guidelines, was common practice. He would tell

Lotan that the police now had evidence sufficient to charge him with the assault of David as well as the thefts, pointedly noting that, if David died, the charge would be murder. In response to Lotan's certain claim of innocence, Clavel would make it clear that such a claim rang hollow given the evidence and the absence of any other suspects.

The strategy worked as predicted.

"You win, Commissaire," said Lotan, taking a deep breath and slumping in his chair. "Yes, I was involved in the theft of the van Dongen, as well as several prior thefts. The van Dongen is the only painting I actually stole. In the earlier cases, I was just a bit player hired by an international network of art thieves to market stolen works. But in *none* of the cases, *none*, have I committed violence," said Lotan, rising and walking to the window with his back turned to Clavel.

"But you didn't oppose others doing so?" asked Clavel.

"Not actively. I didn't encourage it or condone it, but I was powerless to stop it. I knew when we stole the van Dongen painting that the network might find out and demand a cut. They made it clear when I worked with them that they 'owned' the art theft market, and that anyone who tried to take a share would be made to pay."

"But you went ahead with the van Dongen theft anyway," interrupted Clavel.

"Yes, but only because I couldn't do otherwise. Madame Langel's threat to reveal my past crimes was a greater risk."

"Did you suggest to her that the 'network' should be involved?"

"Goodness, no. If I had told her more than she already knew, my fate would have been much, much worse than Monsieur Barber's."

"So they did find out and demand a cut?" asked Clavel.

"Not just a cut, they demanded the entire proceeds from a future sale. They claimed I had jeopardized their entire enterprise, and that the proceeds wouldn't even cover the cost of dealing with the risk. They didn't say what the risk was, or how they planned to deal with it, but I knew the answer to at least the second question when I heard about the break-in."

"So you're convinced the 'network' orchestrated the break-in but have no idea why they thought it necessary?" asked Clavel with obvious skepticism.

"Given the description of what they did, I can only assume they were trying to destroy some evidence David must have uncovered. Why else would they trash the apartment and savagely attack David?"

After being promised police protection and a reduced sentence for the thefts, Lotan provided detailed information about the "network" and its members. As what he termed a "bit player," he had a surprising amount of information. The information was transmitted to Interpol, which took charge of the case.

CHAPTER 56

THE CASE WAS THEN OUT OF CLAVEL'S and his team's hands and they all turned to other issues, all except Jersey. Crime hadn't taken a vacation during the past weeks, and several homicides demanded Clavel and Claire's attention. With both their permissions, Jersey began writing an article he hoped to sell to major U.S. publications. It would be about the Barber case, not about the art mafia. He didn't know enough about that, and anyway that was a piece David should write. If he regained his memory.

Jersey had promised to allow Clavel and Claire to read his article before he sent it out, to be sure he had not included any confidential information. He had no problem with that. In fact, he was glad because it gave him an excuse to remain in Paris, in Claire's apartment.

One afternoon as he was revising his text, the phone rang. It was Claire.

"He remembers."

"What?"

"David has regained his memory, and the doctors say we can speak to him. I'm on my way to the hospital. Meet me there."

When he arrived, he found Claire and David sitting in the two chairs in front of the windows. They were both laughing.

David jumped up and embraced Jersey *à la française,* that is, with the two-cheek kiss.

"My favorite student looks fantastic," exclaimed Jersey, giving him a bear hug.

"And is. Moreover, I'm going to be your favorite investigative reporter," laughed David.

"Oh, yes?"

"Yes. I'm no fool. I emailed copies of all my notes to myself, meaning I can retrieve them on any computer."

"That's probably why they tried to inflict permanent amnesia. I gather the blow was strategically designed to do so," said Claire.

"Well, they failed, and I'm going to publish one hell of a story. You wouldn't believe how extensive the operation is and how successful it's been over the past decade."

"First we have to contact Interpol, and you have to tell them everything you know. Arresting those guys is the first order of business."

"Agreed, but I'm going to publish what I know."

"Only after the arrests are made," Clavel insisted. "If you go public first, it will alert the gang and make arrests that much more difficult."

Claire and Jersey both nodded their agreement. Looking disappointed, David also nodded.

CHAPTER 57

I T WAS ONLY A MATTER OF WEEKS before Interpol had apprehended five members of the "network." And but a few weeks after that when the *New York Times* printed David's article.

Jersey, back in Buffalo making arrangements to move to Paris, immediately called Joe at the *Buffalo News*.

"Yes, I saw it. A good story, and yes, maybe I underestimated David," said Joe before Jersey could say a word.

"Maybe?"

"OK, you have better judgment than I do."

"Thanks. Now will you publish my mediocre piece about the Barber case?"

"Have you seen the paper today?"

"You ran it?"

"Of course, and we thank you for sending it to us and not the *Times*. Your description of the Parisian police team is priceless. Let me take you to lunch tomorrow. I want to discuss your doing a regular column for us."

"It might have to be from a Parisian perspective."

"Why am I not surprised?" laughed Joe. "See you at noon tomorrow—usual place."

Within five minutes, Jersey had David on the phone.

"David, first, congrats on your article. I'm sure you'll be getting a ton of job offers, so I wanted to get my bid in first. The *Buffalo News* has asked me to do a regular column. I'm meeting Joe tomorrow to discuss the possibility. I'd like to propose that you and I do a regular column from Paris. I'd insist that we have a pretty free rein on deciding the topics.

"What do you think?"

"So now I'm no longer *persona non grata* at *Buff News*?"

"Hardly. Joe thought your *Times* piece was prizeworthy, and he admitted he had misjudged you."

"Well, I guess I can afford to generously forgive him," laughed David. "And it would be an honor to work with you. So, yes, I'm game. But not until after the wedding."

CPSIA information can be obtained
at www.ICGtesting.com
Printed in the USA
BVHW082154230221
600893BV00005B/364